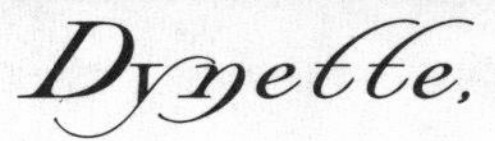

Ann,

Rebecca,

and Emily

MIRA, MIRROR

Mette Ivie Harrison

VIKING

VIKING
Published by Penguin Group
Penguin Young Readers Group, 345 Hudson Street, New York, New York 10014, U.S.A.
Penguin Group (Canada), 10 Alcorn Avenue, Toronto, Ontario, Canada M4V 3B2
(a division of Pearson Penguin Canada Inc.)
Penguin Books Ltd, 80 Strand, London WC2R 0RL, England
Penguin Ireland, 25 St Stephen's Green, Dublin 2, Ireland (a division of Penguin Books Ltd)
Penguin Group (Australia), 250 Camberwell Road, Camberwell, Victoria 3124, Australia
(a division of Pearson Australia Group Pty Ltd)
Penguin Books India Pvt Ltd,
11 Community Centre, Panchsheel Park, New Delhi – 110 017, India
Penguin Group (NZ), Cnr Airborne and Rosedale Roads, Albany, Auckland, New Zealand
(a division of Pearson New Zealand Ltd)
Penguin Books (South Africa)
(Pty) Ltd, 24 Sturdee Avenue, Rosebank, Johannesburg 2196, South Africa
Penguin Books Ltd, Registered Offices: 80 Strand, London WC2R 0RL, England

First published in 2004 by Viking, a division of Penguin Young Readers. Group

3 5 7 9 10 8 6 4 2

Text set in Columbus MT
Book design by Jim Hoover

LIBRARY OF CONGRESS CATALOGING-IN-PUBLICATION DATA
Harrison, Mette Ivie, date–
Mira, Mirror / by Mette Ivie Harrison.
p. cm.
Summary: Long after the disappearance of Snow White's stepmother,
the witch trapped in her mirror manipulates a desperate peasant and a
merchant's daughter to seek the magic she needs to gain her freedom,
but the girls show her a power far greater.
ISBN 0-670-05923-4 (hardcover)
[1. Mirrors—Fiction. 2. Magic—Fiction. 3. Witches—Fiction. 4. Sisters—Fiction.
5. Characters in literature—Fiction. 6. Fairy tales.] I. Title.
PZ8.H248Mi 2004
[Fic]—dc22
2004004132

Prologue

THE BARGAIN was quickly made between my mother and the witch. A half load of rotting firewood for an apprentice. A second apprentice, the witch had said when my mother tried to get more. She had one apprentice already.

Then my mother had gone. The witch waved a hand and told me to acquaint myself with the woods around the hut. She went inside, she said to study a potion. But her roaring snores suggested she was studying her dreams instead.

Still, I was glad to wander. This part of the woods was quiet, and I had had few chances in my life to be away from the noise of my raucous half-brothers.

A few yards past the stream I saw a clearing had been made. There was a girl standing in it over a fire who had to be the witch's other apprentice. Who else would dare to come so near the hut?

When I smelled burned feathers and blood, I assumed

that she was cooking a meal. My mouth began to water and I stepped closer.

The girl was smaller than I, and when I saw her face I was surprised at how handsome she was. She did not look at all like wizened Zerba, whose back and hands were curled with pain, whose face was pocked and scarred. The reverse, in fact. Her black hair glistened in the sun, her eyes were dark and piercing. Her frame, as it turned toward me, was willowy and lithe.

"Good morning," she said.

"My name is Mira," I said. "I'm the new apprentice."

She nodded and smiled a smile full of white, straight teeth. She gave me her name and turned her attention back to the bird on the spit. I realized then that the bird was still alive. Its tiny body struggled as its life dripped into the flames, sizzling and sputtering.

"What are you doing?" I asked, horrified. I had seen animals killed before, but never like this. Even my brothers, who loved the kill, did not torture.

"Taking the magic of its life," she said simply.

"A bird?" Hadn't everyone heard stories of witches going mad from animal magic? My mother had told me of one witch who had taken a hawk's life, then thrown herself off a cliff, as if she could fly.

Then again, my mother had sold me to Zerba. So why should I believe her word?

The other apprentice shrugged. “From whatever is at hand.”

I moved closer, feeling nothing but the heat of the fire. “How do you do it?” I asked, fascinated despite myself.

“If you are near a creature as it dies,” she said, “you can take its magic for your own. But if you want true power, you must take a vibrant life and all its pain.”

I didn’t trust her. She was only an apprentice, after all. I looked back and saw the corner of the hut against the trees. How long until Zerba would appear to teach me real magic?

“Magic is born in life,” said the apprentice. “But it must be taken by death.” She sounded very sure. “So it is and so it will always be.”

I watched as the bird stilled at last. I expected a muttered spell, an incantation. But the other apprentice simply let the bird drop into the fire. Then she took a breath. “There,” she said, dusting off her hands.

She turned toward me slowly, as if to show off a new gown. But the change she had bought from this magic was, in fact, much subtler. It took me several moments to see it: the nose, long and bony before, had become slightly shorter. It was still too long for the rest of her face, but not as obviously as it had been before.

“Ugly as a witch. Might as well be one.” Those were

my mother's last stinging words to me. Yet here was a witch who was anything but ugly.

The other apprentice glanced over my figure—too tall and broad shouldered, my mother had told me often enough. "I could show you how to use magic to change whatever you wish," she offered.

It had been so long since I'd heard anything but criticisms and curses, the kindness seemed too much for me. I went wild with imagination. "Could I have black hair?" I asked, thinking that I had only to copy her to be beautiful.

"If you wish."

"And could you make me smaller, more graceful?"

She sighed, then came over and held my big, ungainly arms above my head, tracing the line of them in her mind. Moving to my back, she ran a finger along the outline of my shoulder blades. When I tried to hunch over, as my mother had encouraged me to hide my height, the other apprentice made a small sound of tongue to teeth and shook her head. She came around front again and lifted my chin so that I was looking straight ahead. Finally, she inched my hips forward, so that they were directly beneath my spine.

Doubtless I looked more like a castle than a princess, but somehow I felt royal where she had touched me. It was not because of any magic she had given me, that I was sure of. I was just as certain that it was not something magic could take away.

"You have your own beauty," she said quietly. "I would not have you imitate anyone else's."

I gaped at her.

"Who was it?" she asked. "Mother? Father? Sister? Brother? Who hurt you so?"

"I never had a sister," I said.

"But the others?" she asked.

I hung my head, thinking how many times I had been told it was my fault, that I had to be punished.

"No," said the apprentice, lifting my chin. "Do not do to yourself what they have always done to you. Here you are free to become whatever you will."

I said nothing. I liked her voice far better than mine.

"You only need magic," she said softly.

"Will you show me how?" I asked.

She gestured at the bird on the ground. "That is the beginning. But follow me and there will be no end to your power."

"What of Zerba?" I asked.

"Zerba takes her magic from graveyards and animals ready for slaughter. Such easy magic gives her cures for headaches, love spells, and wart removers." The apprentice said it with distaste, as though she were listing the tasks of a village gravedigger. "But I will teach you far more. Unless your vision is as limited as hers."

"No, no," I said. In fact, my vision had been exactly

that limited. But it was beginning to swell.

"Then you will learn from me." With a pleased expression, she patted my shoulder. "We will work together, you and I, Mira."

"I—work with you?" I had no idea how I could contribute to the project, since she was the one with all the knowledge. "How?"

"Before you kill a fish to eat for dinner, bring it to me. I will make sure its life is not wasted. And if you ever have the need to kill something larger—I will help you. Old lovers, bullies, enemies from the past—you can profit doubly from their deaths. Provided you share the profit with me. Do you understand?"

"Yes," I said, not understanding at all. "Of course."

"Good." She came close to me, brushing her shoulder against my lower arm, taking my hand in hers. Her voice was so sweet it overwhelmed the smell of dead bird. "Then we will be sisters, you and I."

"Sisters?" I hardly dared say it, for fear I had mistaken her.

I had not.

"I will be the older, wiser sister," she said.

The beautiful sister, I thought.

"You will be the younger sister, eager to assist me, eager to learn and to grow."

It was all I could ask for. I would have skipped around

the fire if my mother had not told me how gawky I looked when I did that. "Thank you," I said. "Oh, thank you."

I thought that day was the end of my heartache. It was but the beginning.

Years passed. Zerba died. Her hut became my sister's. My sister's shelter was mine. I had hardly changed from the gawky girl I had been. But my sister's long, raven black hair was now only one breathtaking feature among many. Her face was perfectly balanced, her skin flawless. Her neck would have made a swan swim away in shame. Her fingers tapered to long nails that clicked music when she moved them. There was nothing about her that had not been worked over with precise magic.

I asked her once who the beauty was for. It seemed a waste to share it only with the forest, and me.

She laughed at me and told me not to worry about waste. "I have plans for my beauty," she said. "Plans for my magic, and for you too. Great plans."

"Oh?" I waited for her to share them with me.

It was a long wait. After Zerba was gone, fewer villagers came to ask us for our magic. They were afraid of my sister, and who could blame them? There were rumors about missing cattle, horses, and even a child or two. Those who braved her despite the rumors found her cruel and dismissive.

She would not be bothered for such petty requests as a curse on a neighbor or a blessing for a sickly newborn. And I did not blame her. Her magic was more than any of us deserved.

Yet when I offered the villagers my magic, it always turned wrong. A potion to cure the pox seemed to spread the disease instead. Half the village died, and only the most desperate returned to me. They had little left to pay me with, but I took it for my sister's sake. She hardly ate, and whatever magic she worked for beauty, it would not keep her alive. I did not feel that I had much to offer her, but all that I had, I gave.

Year after year I gave, until one beautiful cloudless summer day, my sister returned at last from a two-day trip. I hurried to her as soon as she called for me, ducking my head to enter her hut. I had brought her favorites, stewed rabbit and fried mushrooms from the forest.

She took no notice of the food, however. "Do you see this?" My sister held in her hand a mirror the size and shape of a face.

I came close enough to see the warmth in the polished color of the wood and the intricate carving around the glass. It was not a large mirror, however. "It is as beautiful as you are," I said, at last.

"Take hold of it. Feel its power." She thrust the mirror at me.

I saw no reason not to do as she asked. It was only

after I touched the whorled wood against my skin, sensed the magic, bitter and smelling of old smoke, of death, that I began to feel a hint of fear.

"I told you I had plans for you, Mira." Her voice was soft and delicate, but I felt like the bird squirming above the fire as it burned to death to give her power. But why? What had I ever done to deserve this?

"I have been waiting for the right mirror. A queen's mirror."

What queen? I tried to open my mouth, but it seemed I had no lips to open, no tongue to form words, no throat to make sound, no lungs to give me breath. The only sound that came from me was that of breaking glass. And then the sound again, in reverse. The glass, once shattered, had reformed itself.

What had happened? I looked to my sister for help, but my neck was so stiff that my view of her was limited to a small circle—no more than that. I began to realize I had changed. I had become something that could not move.

"Do not worry, Mira. You will be with me still. You will help your older sister, as you always have. Only now your sister will be a queen."

A queen's mirror, she had said. Her mirror, then? But how?

"Do you not wish to know your part, little sister? I

will need you at my side for every step. But first, take this," she said, and sent magic to me.

It was water to my thirst, and I drank it in, then gasped. I made a croaking sound and realized my voice had returned. "What plans?" I asked. I still trusted her, you see.

"Who is a queen? The wife of a king, of course," she answered herself, before I could. "And who does a king marry?" She looked into me, admiring herself in my glass. "The fairest in the land," she said. "And you, Mira, will make sure that I am always the fairest in the land."

Did it take so long? Yes, it did. For it was only at this moment that my trust for her began to die.

Perhaps she sensed it, for she turned her attention to placating me. As if it mattered. "Mira, do not be angry with me. I wanted to keep you by my side forever. We are sisters, you see."

I had never thought it terrible before, but it was then.

"And in a way, what I have given you is a great gift. The gift of eternal life. Now we will never be parted. You can never leave me. And I, of course, would never leave you." She put her hand to the wood that surrounded me and stroked it gently.

I shivered.

"And it is only fair that you must change, for I must change too. And I need your help, Mira. Will you help me?"

I did not answer her.

"Mira." There was a strain in her voice. "My magic has bought me beauty bit by bit, but a queen's mirror has special powers. With a witch inside of it, it can make marvelous changes, if only it has the magic. I will give you the magic. I have proved it already, have I not?" She put a hand to her heart.

If she had a heart and had not taken it out, still beating, to sacrifice to her magic.

"I do not ask much of you, Mira. Only this one thing, in return for all that I have given you. And perhaps someday, I will turn you back into yourself. If you do well, Mira. If you do well," she crooned.

But still I did not answer her.

I could see the anger in her before I felt it. Her hands shook with the magic, then it passed to me, warm at first, then gradually hotter and hotter. My wood began to smoke from it. The pain rose, and I cannot describe what it was like in human terms. It might have been a stake in my eye. It might have been a dagger to my breast. It might have been the jaws of a great beast on my arm.

"Speak to me, Mira," said my sister. "Tell me you will do as I say. Tell me you will be happy."

The pain went on and on, and I struggled against it. But what was I against her? Not even a younger sister anymore. Only a mirror.

"I am content," I said. No more than that.

But it was enough for my sister. She sighed, then removed her hands from me and set me aside. "I am glad. Now we can begin."

And she told me what to do. How to change the smell of her, so that no one would guess she had ever been a witch. How to change her eyes, her nose, her chin to a different perfection. And last of all, how to make her taller and rounder—almost as I had been, once upon a time.

"Yes," said my sister. "Yes. This will do. For now. You will learn more, Mira, and then I will be a queen. For now, I will practice being a duchess, and see what men I can lure to my trap."

She left me feeling drained and bitter. The magic she had given me she had taken back. She might give me more another day, but how long would I keep it? A day? An hour? I doubted very much she would ever leave me a chance to turn the magic back on myself. And I did not know even if it would work.

Could a mirror transform itself back into a human? Or would I stay forever in this prison, waiting for a mercy I was sure my sister had never had?

I wanted to weep for myself, but a mirror made of glass and wood cannot weep real tears. Not with all the magic in the world.

Chapter One

"MIRROR, MIRROR, on the wall. Make me the fairest one of all."

It was the queen's constant demand, but there came a day she did not speak it. She did not come from the castle to the hideaway in the forest where she kept her secret magics. She told me she would go after the little princess she hated, the one who had a natural beauty to exceed even the queen's unnatural one. The queen thought her magic must win in the end, but she never returned. I could only assume that she was dead.

Year after year I hung there. In the beginning, I kept myself alive by taking from what I could see. The magic cauldron, which had been made to keep bubbling, soon stopped. The swirling crystal ball the queen had used to see distant places went black and cold. The magic light dancing above my head went still.

I even took from a passing fly that had been caught in a spiderweb in the corner by me. And a beetle, overcome by its load. But things of magic lose power day by day. It is the same law of nature that bleeds death constantly to the sky, so that it will be gathered again in new life. And so, after fifty years, I had hardly more than my voice.

By the time I heard the first footsteps in the forest outside the shaky stone walls, I called out in desperation, "Please, come. Anyone, help me."

A warrior came out of the forest, his beard grizzled and graying. "Maiden?" he called. "Where is the maiden who called for me?"

"Here I am," I said, my voice trembling as my glass could not.

He searched for me, found me at last, and then tightened his lips. There was hatred in his eyes, though I knew of no reason why he should hate me. Stories told by dwarves, perhaps, of a magic mirror used by a horrible queen?

But I did not have time to ask him, for I saw his ax begin its ascent. I acted quickly, using the last of my magic on his face. The sight of his own grandfather looking back at him gave him a sudden fright. He stumbled on a crack in the warped wooden floor, then fell forward and cut his own head open.

It was fortunate for me that he died, and quickly, so that he did not have time to escape. I needed magic to replace what I had lost. So I listened to the gurgling of the blood draining his life from him and took it to myself. It was not as powerful as it would have been had the queen killed him herself, as she so often did. But he had been surprised by his death, and that was enough.

In the months following, the warrior's bones were taken by wild creatures and scattered through the forest. Only his skull remained in the far corner where it had rolled in a driving rain that broke through the roof above him. Perhaps I should have pitied him his nameless end. As a warrior, he had trained all his days to die gloriously in battle. Instead he had died to give a magic mirror power to hope for another twenty years, if she was stingy with her use.

It was a gypsy who came next. Just when I was ready to think my chances were over, I saw her tall, thin form through the broken window. She was nearly the same size as the queen, and for a moment I had a start of hope that the queen was not dead, that she had come back for me after all. Then I saw the rags she wore, and the cane she hobbled with. The queen had gone in disguise now and then, but surely not like this.

"There is magic here," said the gypsy, sniffing

along the outer edge of bricks. "I feel it."

If she could sense magic, I thought, perhaps she was a witch herself.

"Here," I called. "On the wall. The mirror."

The gypsy found her way in, then moved forward. She did not mistake which piece in the room still had magic. Lifting a gnarled hand to brush the ivy from my face, she sighed with pleasure. "Ah. You will make a fine piece at a fair. No other fortune-teller will have a talking mirror."

A fair? A fortune-teller? Now that she was full in my vision, I could taste all her magic. It was not much. A few chickens, no doubt, stolen from a nearby farm. And from the smell of her breath, the unhatched eggs eaten raw as well.

But unlike my sister, who had been queen, I was in no position to be particular with my magic. I would have to take what I could get.

The gypsy chuckled softly to herself. "Pretty, pretty. Good luck to find you. Yes, yes."

Good luck, indeed. But not hers.

I stole from her quietly at first, but soon she began to shriek at me, threatening to break my glass. I had to protect myself. So I used her own magic to wither the hand hovering near me. The gypsy howled in pain, but she did not retreat.

I blinded her in one eye next. I could have taken both,

but I did not have to. Moaning and mindless, she lurched away from me. The broken section of the wall she had come through crumbled further as she slammed against it. When she was gone at last, she had left behind nothing but the echo of her powerless curses.

I was alone again, and I must fend for myself. I saved as much magic as I could for the future, and then I waited.

A hundred years I waited.

In the dying sunlight of what might have been my last spring, I saw a shadow of a girl huddled under the bushes near the ruined window. She had no magic in her, but she was just young enough for me to deceive and just desperate enough for me to help.

She would have to do. I did not have time to wait for another. So I made a sound like a grunting bear, and projected it toward her.

The girl jerked up, holding her arms around herself and searching for the animal who had made the noise.

Finally, she saw the outline of the queen's hideaway. She peered through the open window, her shoulders poking through the tatters of her shift. Then she lifted a leg onto the sill, crouched for a moment, and let herself fall inward. She landed on a soft pile of moss in the corner and looked with wide eyes through the room where the queen's magic had been so strong. Nothing left of it now but me.

It was too dark for her to see me clearly, but she nestled her head down, and shortly I could hear the sound of deep, even breaths that meant sleep. Well, I could wait until morning if need be. What was one more night among thousands? It would only give me more time to plan. After all, once I had persuaded her to help me, I had to decide where to lead her for my magic. It drained me further, to taste the faint scents on the air. But in the end, I knew which direction to go.

There were wars aplenty and masses dying of disease anywhere, but I needed more powerful magic. As a mirror, I would have few chances to kill for myself. And perhaps I was still too much the soft child I had been in the beginning to do it alone. But if the girl took me to the right place, I could surely find a way. I did not know if there was one great witch ahead or many smaller ones, but even a great witch sometimes had a use for money, and smaller witches could be fooled.

It was morning by then, and I saw the sun had risen to dapple the girl's face black and gold. Delicate and smooth underneath the grime, her features reminded me of the queen's when she had been young. The only difference was the uncertainty. The queen had never been uncertain.

Nor was I. "Hello?" I called.

The girl startled awake and hopped to her feet, staring around.

"Here," I said. "On the wall. Beneath the vines."

She turned in my direction. Her eyes narrowed. She took a step. She saw herself in my glass, put a hand up to her nose and felt across the swelling, the one flaw in what might otherwise have been a perfect face.

"I can help you," I offered.

But at the sound of my voice, the girl ducked down low to the ground, holding her face to her knees, as if to protect it from blows. Scuttling, she tried to move back toward the corner where she had been safe, for a little while.

"You need not be afraid of me," I said, as patiently as I could manage.

The girl let her head peek out from between her knees for one moment, no more. Then she covered it again, as if not seeing her fate would save her from it.

"I am a magic mirror. I will not hurt you."

"Magic?" She looked afraid.

I guessed that she had heard stories of how magic was won, as I had before I had come to Zerba. "Small magic," I said to reassure her.

She did not move, and I realized I needed to bait her. "Enough to change your face," I tried.

It was enough. She came closer to me, her back not quite straight. When she looked at me this time, it was not to see herself. "Change my face? So that no one could recognize me?" she asked eagerly.

"Your father, you mean?" I asked.

Her eyes grew round with wonder, as if I had shown her the most magnificent magic instead of simple deductive skills. Who else would have hurt her, so that she learned to walk in a crouch? Who else would have taught her to speak in a near-whisper at all times? And who but the man who reigned at home would have forced her from it?

But perhaps I guessed too well. She turned suspicious in a moment. "If you know of my father, then how do I know he did not send you here himself?" she demanded.

I doubted her father had enough imagination to think of using his left hand to hit her when his right grew sore. But I would go at it slowly, if she wished. "I only guessed it was he who hurt you because I have heard of fathers who beat their daughters. It is a common enough tale among humans. That is all."

It was more than a tale for me. My own father, or rather the man I was forced to call "Father," had been nothing to me and became less. In the ten years since he had moved into our hut, he made my mother's belly swell five times. The two girls had died in their sleep before they were a few days old. The three boys had lived, each more loud and demanding and more like his father than the one before. I had been glad to be rid of them all by the time I was sold to Zerba the witch.

"I ran away from him," said the girl, as if challenging me to tell her she was wrong.

I had no intention of it. I had run away myself, but I had always been found. Found and brought back for another beating.

"I won't go back," she insisted.

"Good." She would be no use if she were the kind of girl who only ran away because she hoped to be brought home.

"You can change my face?" All fear of magic had disappeared in her need.

"Of course," I said. "But first, you must take me down from the wall." I had the most delicious anticipation of how it would feel to be free at last from the rough brick behind me.

The girl reached, but the ivy had grown so thick that it now held me tight to the wall.

"Cut through the vines." I wished the girl had a knife, but she had come with nothing but hope.

Grunting, she ripped through the ivy with her hands. The wall trembled. The vines had been holding the bricks too. Not long now and the whole place would be dust, forgotten as I was.

"Now lift me," I said. "There is a hole at the top of my wood." It was like a knot in my neck, and when she lifted me off it, the strain was suddenly gone. I could feel the air circulating all around me, and in the hands that touched mine, the pump of a beating heart. I would have smiled if I could. "Thank you," I said instead.

I did not have to tell her to go outside. She went eagerly, stepping around the rubble.

"Toward the stream," I directed.

She held me tucked under one arm like a babe in a blanket, and when we came to the stream, she stopped and dabbed cool water on my glass, wiping it clean. When she was finished, she held me up so that the sun made a ball of white fire in me.

Then she cleaned her own face, wincing as she touched the tender parts of skin. "Now," she said, putting me down on the bank beside her. "Change me."

But I had no intention of wasting my magic so soon. "Don't you think we should be on our way first?" I asked. "We do not want to be here, after all, should your father come for you. New face or not, he may recognize you by your manners. Or take you back to his hut even if he does not recognize you." It was cruel to use her fear so, but I had learned cruelty from a fine teacher.

"Where should we go, then?" she asked, turning her face in a half circle around the stream.

I took a moment to sense for magic. Then I decided. "South," I said. "And west."

"Which way is south?" the girl asked, staring about the forest bewilderedly. "Which way is west?"

Of course, she knew nothing about the world except for the village she had grown up in. "Deeper into the forest," I said. "Following the stream."

She picked me up, willing to be led, at least for now. "All right then. We will go."

I was not heavy, but I had no handle, so I was difficult to hold in one hand. The girl held me in two instead, and I jogged from side to side as she ran. It was near midday when she stopped, her face so red I thought it would burst into flames.

She dipped her hand into the stream for water, and splashed it over her face first, then into her mouth. "He won't come this far, will he?" she asked.

I hesitated. She looked at the end of her strength, but I could not afford to allow her to feel free of her father. She would begin to focus on other things, like the magic I had not yet proven to her I had. "We can rest for a time, at least," I said, in compromise.

She eased herself down by the stream and caught her breath. "It is the horse he wants," she said, after a time. "Not me."

"The horse?" I did not understand.

"Old Vanye promised my father a horse if we were married. My father thought it wonderful that he need pay no dowry and would still be rid of the need to feed me."

She held me closer to her stomach, and I caught a glimpse of the ribs under her shift. Whatever her father had fed her, it was not much.

"And you did not wish to marry old Vanye," I guessed.

"He is as old as my father's father," said the girl. "His grandson is nearly twenty. If the grandson had offered for me, perhaps I would have considered it—" But she was already shaking her head. "No. I have seen the way he treats his animals. He would have been no better than my father, or old Vanye."

She dangled her feet in the water and looked at me. She did not see her own face, though. It was as if she were looking for mine.

My eyes, my nose, my cheeks and chin—all long lost.

"The priest came, and I would not say yes. My father took me away and said that he would convince me. The others all waited. The priest. Old Vanye. The grandson."

I remembered my father beating me, inviting my

brothers to join in. I remembered my mother looking away. That was the worst of it, knowing that no one would help me. This girl knew the same.

But I pushed away the sympathy I felt. I had no room for it in me now. If I felt for this peasant girl, I would lose the determination I needed to force her to my will. And then it would be she using me, as the queen had used me, year after year. Until the day came when I forgot what it was like to even wish to be human.

"He beat me until I pretended I had fainted. Then he went away, to bring me ale, and the priest. That was when I ran." She spoke matter-of-factly, with the courage that comes from a hard life.

"Girl," I said. But of course I could not speak to her that way. A name would matter to her. "What are you called?"

"Ivana," she said with a shrug. And then she added, "I was named for my father."

Not much of a name, but she could take another, if she wished it. When I had decided it was time for the change. I waited for her to get up from the stream, but she bit at her lower lip and stared into me.

"What is it?" I asked. "What do you need?" I thought it would be a request that I use my magic on food.

She surprised me, however, and it was not for the last time. "What about your name?"

My name? "I do not need a name," I said. When I was human again, perhaps.

"Oh." She looked chastened. Then suddenly, she brightened. "I will call you 'Mirror.'" She nodded to herself in satisfaction.

And why should I complain? It was what I was.

Chapter Two

I GUIDED IVANA'S trudging feet onward. The farther into the forest we went, the more magic I sensed. I had no idea how much it was, or how far apart the witches who had gathered it were. I did not know if it was guarded, either, though I guessed much of it would be. Well, I would find out more as we got closer.

We had begun in the brightness of morning, but the thick canopy of trees dimmed the light. We kept close to the stream, which grew ever wider and faster as it was added to by rivulets here and there. In some places, there was no room between the water and the trees it fed, so Ivana had to walk directly in the cold sluice.

Once she fell over a jagged stone. She lurched forward, and I was sure she would let me fall to the rocks to save herself. Instead, her right hand plucked me from my warm spot under her arm and held me high, behind her head.

Without care for anything but me, she landed on her face.

I heard a sharp intake of breath, but no other complaint of pain. She clambered out of the stream and sat on the shore, cupping cold water in her hands to staunch the bleeding. Her nose was swollen to the size of a hen's egg, and there was a long cut that ran from one red eye to her chin.

But it was me she showed concern for. "I did not break you?" she asked, examining my every inch.

"No," I said.

She breathed deeply and looked to the black bits of sky poking through the branches. It was far into night, but Ivana continued until she was past exhausted. I should have stopped her earlier, but my sense of time as a mirror was different from what it had been when I was human. Without the queen, it was hard for me to be sure exactly how much time had passed.

I remembered once when the queen had left me alone. She did not say when she came back where she had been, though I could guess easily enough that she had gone to gather death, for she was full of new magic. And from the clothes she threw in the fire, it smelled as though it were some place poor and crowded and easy to buy pain.

"How long have you been away?" I asked her. I had lost so much of what it was to be human. I did not want to lose all sense of time, as well.

But she answered me flippantly. "Long enough that I will be able to finish what I have begun here."

"You look older," I said, trying to irritate her enough to get her attention.

It worked. The queen whirled, her hand raised. There was a ring on it that I had seen her use before, a great ruby ring in the shape of a heart, though to think it was a sign of softness in her would be a terrible mistake. The bottom of the heart had been used before, honed to an edge as sharp as any dagger.

I had seen the effects of that edge on human flesh. What would it do to me, a mirror? I could only guess that it would not be pleasant. But she contained her anger before I found out.

"If I look older," she said, her voice high and strained, but in control—always in control—"I only need to ask you to ease the signs." She held a hand out and gave me her magic.

I was starved for it and ate it up. I would have taken all she had, but she drew back and set her guards again before I had any more than she wished to give. Then she laughed. "Greedy little mirror," she said. "It is not time for that yet. A few more years, perhaps."

I was long past believing her, and yet I could not throw away the hope entirely, or I would have refused to do anything she asked. While she lived, and I did, there was still a chance. It was all I had.

So she stood in front of me and I smoothed away the wrinkles on her forehead, lifted the sagging flesh under her chin, and flattened the swelling around her eyes.

"My nose," she said, pointing.

It had begun to grow again. It did that, day by day. I reduced the size and firmed the shape of it.

She breathed a sigh of relief, but I saw her rubbing against the inside of the ring, as though the thought of using it to cut me still tempted her.

"I only wanted to know how many days you were away," I said meekly.

"How many days? What do you care? You will never show signs of age as I do." She peered into me, seeing her sister, I think, for the first time in many years. "I am half jealous of you for that."

"I would trade you places if you wish," I said, daring her to offer. Of course, she did not.

"Ah, but what would you do as a queen?" she asked, twisting my pain to nothing. "You would waste all I have built up, I am afraid. And—" She smiled that smile that I hated now. "I think I would not make as good a mirror as you. I fear I would always be wanting to escape. Not like my dear sweet sister, always waiting to help me instead."

"You won't tell me how long I waited to help you this

time?" It was not quite begging, but near enough to the prisoners brought before the queen that I cringed to hear it come from me.

"A month, two months? It does not matter now," said the queen.

And she would say no more on the matter.

Ivana tripped over the root of a gnarled oak tree and brought me back to the present. I realized that she was walking like a drunken man, with no sense of direction. It would do me no good to keep her going this way. She would hurt herself, or me, or she would get us hopelessly lost.

"It is time to stop for the night," I said. She was the one I should think of now, not the queen, for Ivana was my future and the queen was my past.

"I can go on," said Ivana stubbornly.

"No," I said, borrowing the queen's imperious voice for once. I liked the sound of it, the throb of it in my glass. I liked Ivana's reaction even more.

She did not take another step but simply sank to the ground.

"Sleep," I said.

She found a soft hollow of grass to set me in. Then she closed her eyes and snored noisily through the night.

I thought how easy it was to forget the need to sleep. Now, the dreaming—that I had not forgotten. How it had been to dream of good food, of love and laughter. Then to wake fresh from the night to the sight of dawn in the morning sky—and everything of which I had dreamed. Yes. That was why I wished to be human again. All the disadvantages of a human body meant nothing in comparison to that.

Then near morning I felt a deluge of tiny drops of water. It took me a moment to recognize what it was. Rain. Since becoming a mirror, I had been protected in the queen's hideaway against the vagaries of weather. I searched for old memories of rain, but none of them had been like this. Nothing was the same in my wood and glass shell.

A rim formed around my left side, between the lip of my wood and my glass. Ivana stirred, saw my plight, and shook the water from me. "I am sorry," she said sleepily. "I should have found a better place for you."

The sound of an apology was as strange as the feel of the water. Who would apologize to a mirror? Who but a peasant girl named Ivana?

"Will you rot?" she asked then, her eyes anxious and blurry in my glass. "Will you lose your magic?"

"I was well made," I said shortly. "It would take a hundred years of damp and cold for me to feel a bit of wet." I could say that much good of the queen—she had not trapped me in a badly made mirror. I was well sealed.

Ivana stretched and yawned. Her nose was healing quickly, from both the break and the fall. It hardly seemed swollen at all now. Certainly, she paid no attention to it. She stood up and found a tree to relieve herself behind privately. I felt a moment's surprise at the courtesy. She treated me as if I were a traveling companion, rather than a magic object she intended to use and then discard.

Well, she would not do the discarding. "I suppose you are hungry, as well," I said tartly.

"Yes," said Ivana, and she apologized yet again, then picked me up off the forest floor and carried me to the bank of the stream. She put her hands into the water, held them very still, and waited.

I thought how much like me she was, waiting for her prey as I had waited on the wall for mine. Then in an instant, before the fish knew what had happened, Ivana had snatched it into her hands and held it triumphantly above the water.

Its scales were silver in the sun, its eyes white and knowing. A fish is made to die, but this one would die a little sooner than the rest. Ivana stepped toward the edge of the water, focusing on a good-sized, dry rock.

"Wait!" I shouted as she raised the fish.

Ivana turned. Had she not been holding the fish with both hands, she would have lost it as it flopped to one side in a last, desperate hope for freedom.

"I need to see it," I said, telling myself I could not afford the queen's old snobbishness concerning magic.

"Why?" Ivana asked.

"Do I question which fish you choose to grab at?" I asked scathingly. "Or which tree you decide to sleep under?"

Ivana shook her head.

"Then trust me when it comes to magic."

She stared at the fish, a faint look of disgust growing on her face. As if it were better to let the magic go for naught than to take it in. As if I were more bloodthirsty than she, simply because I would consume the fish's life rather than its flesh.

Still, she did as I asked. She found a different rock, upstream from the first. Not as large, nor as flat. But this one I could see. And the fish died all the same when she whacked its head just so. I hardly heard the sound of the brain being smashed, for I was too concentrated on taking the magic from it.

Afterward, I wondered if it had been worth it. Such small magic from that fish. And now Ivana knew how the power of magic was gained. It took practice, but there was no reason she could not do it for herself, if she wished. Ah, I thought, but she wouldn't wish it. Though I had not known her long, I did not believe that Ivana would kill easily. When she was hungry, yes. But not for mere power.

"Do you need a fire?" I asked, thinking to appease her.

"No," she said, and to prove it, she ate the fish raw. She had no knife to open its guts, so she used her teeth instead. She ate the head whole, then ripped the spine from the back and opened the pink flesh.

When she was finished, she lay down on the rock she had killed the fish on, and leaned forward into the stream. She dipped her hands into the water and cupped it to her mouth. The fish in the water slipped by her easily, never knowing how close they had come to death.

We walked on through another day, and stopped when it turned night.

"How much farther?" asked Ivana.

"Not much more," I said. And indeed, the next day we reached a road through the forest. I could feel magic teasing me ahead. There was no way of knowing yet if I would need money or something else. But it was there, waiting for me.

"Are you ready to be changed?" I asked Ivana.

In answer, she closed her eyes, holding very still. As if that would help me.

I waited long enough for her to realize I had done nothing. Then I asked, "What will you do when I change you?" I would not have her disappear after I had spent my magic on her, so I had to make her believe she would need me still as much as I needed her.

Ivana's eyes fluttered open. She stared at me curiously. "What do you mean?"

"Where will you go?" I asked.

Ivana waved a hand vaguely. "There must be a village ahead," she said. "I will find it."

"And in the village, then what?" I pressed. I meant this to be a lesson for her.

"I will ask for work," she said.

"Will you get it? On the first day?"

"No," she admitted. "Likely not."

"Then where will you sleep?" I pounded the questions at her. "Who will give you food? How will you find the strength to work without it?"

She shrunk back, as if my words were blows.

I felt monstrous, as though I had become no better than her father. But what else could I do?

"I don't know," Ivana said. "I don't know." She slumped to the ground, her hands rubbing at her head.

"Perhaps you should not try to enter a village here, then." A gentle suggestion. One gentleness in all the rest.

"Go home, is that what you mean? Go back to my father?" She was overwrought.

"No, not back to your father." I let the words float between us, like magic untaken from a dead body. "But once you have a new face, there is no reason you must remain a peasant."

"What else would I be?" asked Ivana.

A good question. I would answer it. I looked at the ruts dug into the dried mud of the previous night's rain. Next to them were footsteps, deep and crossed on top of one another. There was a tale told in mud, if one knew how to read it. A tale that might well save my magic for another day.

A merchant's wagon had been overtaken by bandits here, I told Ivana. It had been pushed off the road. The goods had been taken, the merchant and his passengers, as well. Perhaps his daughter.

"Oh, we must find her," said Ivana. She stood up in one swift movement. "She will need help."

"No!" Finding the real merchant's daughter was the last thing we needed.

"But why? Do you think she will punish me? She will think I helped the robbers? But I did not. You know I did not."

"You do not understand," I said. "You will be the merchant's daughter."

"Me? How?" She thought for a moment. "Do you mean you will change me to look like her? What does she look like? Have you seen her?" She turned around, as if looking for the body.

"No," I said. "Ivana, listen carefully. I do not need to change your face for you to pretend to be her. Those who will help you have never seen her, after all. The real merchant's daughter, that is."

"But who will help me?" asked Ivana.

"Wait and see," I said. She turned and looked up the road, and I looked with her. It was not a well-cared-for road, but it was well traveled. Surely that would give us some choice. And if the first wagon that came by was not right, we would try again. And again.

Chapter Three

"YOU MUST wait at the bend in the road," I told Ivana. "And hide yourself until another merchant's wagon comes down the road."

She walked to the bend. There was a good place for hiding, behind a large fallen oak. I suspected from the remains of a fire I saw there that this was where the robbers had hidden to take the first merchant. Another bit of luck, which we could take advantage of now.

"Like this?" asked Ivana.

I told her to let my glass lean past the rock so that I could view the road. "Yes," I told her. "Now, for the story of the bandits who have killed your father and taken your inheritance and left you with nothing but your innocence."

Ivana's brow wrinkled. She knew as well as I did that innocence was the last thing a band of thieves was likely to leave a merchant's daughter with. And yet this part was important, for a soiled merchant's daughter might not be taken in.

"I will have to think of a reason they have not touched me. I hid myself, or overcame one of them in battle. A small one, perhaps. A boy."

The words brought another memory of my sister, and of a small boy no higher than my knee, with hair that might have been blond had it not been so dirty. His nose was broken and had healed badly, off to one side. A legacy of a fight with his older brother, no doubt.

It was the older brother who had come to ask my sister for a love spell. She told him how much it would cost him, and he agreed to the price eagerly. Too eagerly. We should have known it was a trick, but it was the first time either of us had had a chance to deal magic alone since Zerba died.

My sister went into the hut to endow a small charm with the magic necessary. Then she came out, holding a broken nut shell on a string. She handed it to the older brother, whose name was Simus. "Put it around your neck and tell it the name of the girl," my sister explained to him.

"What if I don't know her name?" he asked.

"Then think of her. Make sure it is a clear image."

"Do I close my eyes?"

"If you wish."

He closed his eyes. The little brother—I never knew his name—had found a stick and was using it as a sword against a tree. The sword was loud enough, but the boy made additional noise with his mouth, simulating both sides of a full battle.

"How long does it take to work?" asked Simus.

My sister did not answer. "No time—" I began for her. Then I turned and saw her, saw the stupid look on her face, and realized what Simus had done. It was my sister whom he had thought of. He hadn't even needed her name.

Simus leaned closer, put his lips to hers. Instead of fighting him, my sister's arms went around his shoulders and pulled him closer. Simus made a satisfied sound low in his throat, bent to her shoulder, and began to kiss her soft, white skin.

I put a hand on Simus's arm, tried to pull him away. He knocked me back with hardly a thought. I felt the blood trickling down my chin, and it was then I thought of my magic. I used a finger to twist Simus to the left, then to the right.

My sister watched dully until I thought to send magic to her, and she came to herself with a sound of a slap. Her cheeks red and flushed, she took a step forward and tried to add her magic to mine. I pushed it away. I had sufficient for this, and I was angry. I wanted to do it myself.

I cannot say I meant to kill Simus, but I cannot say I meant him to live, either. My magic flung him into the stream, and he landed with his head on a large stone. The stream turned briefly pink, then washed away Simus's blood. The small boy hurried to his older brother's side, but there was no life left to save.

At the realization of what I had done, my stomach churned, and its contents emptied onto the dirt outside the hut. By the time I looked up, my sister had sated her anger on the small body of Simus's younger brother. I saw as his mouth opened to cry out in pain. But it was too late. My sister's magic had caught him, and she would not let go.

The small body melted agonizingly slowly. His head sloughed off into the stream first, making a sound like a falling apple. Then his shoulders slumped into his chest. His hands fell off at the wrist. And at last, the bare torso tipped forward and was washed over. A few more moments of a lump of flesh, and then he was gone.

I found myself back on my knees, vomiting blood and saliva, which was all my stomach held. It made a small pink stream of its own, which trickled past the rock and joined the other.

"He was only a child," I said to my sister when I got to my feet once more and met her at the water's edge, where she looked over her handiwork with satisfaction.

"He would have grown into a man," she answered coldly. "Like his brother."

"You don't know that. He could have grown to be kind and good. He could have been of use in this world."

My sister told me what she thought of that by spitting into the stream.

I began to shake with reaction then. My sister helped me into the hut and gave me some tea. Though her hands felt cruel and pointed at my sides, I let her.

"How old do you think he was?" I asked, my hands shaking around the cup. "Four years? Five?" I thought of my foster brothers. Would I have felt so much for them if I saw them dead?

"Why do you think his brother brought him?" my sister asked, her voice far calmer than mine.

"Because—because—" I had no answer.

"Because he was training him. As a father brings his son hunting to see how it is done, as a mother shows her daughter how to make a fire—so that monster was teaching the younger one to be the same."

"Well, then, he could have been untaught. If he had had a chance." In my mind, it was a shout, but my ears heard only a whisper.

"Did you plan to unteach him yourself?" asked my sister.

"No," I admitted. I would not have known where to

start. "But couldn't he have returned home?"

"And who do you think taught Simus?"

This was a good question. I thought on it a long time, for months afterward, whenever I saw a child from the village with a parent, or a cub with a mother bear, a bird bringing food to her nest.

Perhaps my sister was right. And yet I still thought that he had been only a boy. A small boy.

Ivana stared at me, waiting for an answer to a question I had not heard. Then she gave up in despair. "No, you're right. A merchant will never believe I am anything but a peasant girl." She sighed.

I launched back into my present difficulties with hardly a moment's pause. I thought I could guess easily enough what Ivana feared. "If you were too clean," I said sharply, "he would not feel sorry for you."

But Ivana could not be content with that. "What of my ways?" she asked.

"At first, he will likely think any ignorance you show is because you are still dazed from the battle," I suggested. "After that, you will have learned enough to pass." I hoped this was true, at least. I could not afford careless mistakes. I had a little seed magic, but not much.

Time passed. It grew colder as clouds filled the sky.

"I am afraid," said Ivana, her teeth chattering. "I should go to a village. I should be among peasants. That is where I belong."

Where she belonged, yes. Where I belonged, no. I obviously would have to spend some time reassuring her. "You have met merchants before, have you not?" I asked.

"Seen them," said Ivana. "Spoken a few words, I suppose."

"Well, then, all you must do is to copy what you saw and heard. If they suspect anything is wrong in your manner or your speech, you will say that you are from the far north, and that will explain all."

"But my clothes—?" she asked.

Well, they were not even castoffs of a merchant's daughter, but they were so dirty and torn I doubted anyone would look closely to check the weave. "You must trust me," I insisted. I knew I sounded like my sister when she had tried to convince me killing the boy was right, but I wondered if she felt any of the doubt I did.

Ivana breathed and breathed again. Eventually, she was so quiet I hardly noticed her.

The afternoon passed, and it turned to evening. A drizzle came with the dimming of the sky. It was spring, the season of soft rain, and I did not have the magic to change that. It was some satisfaction to remember that even the queen had not known how to change winter to summer. It had irritated her more than once when she had prepared a spectacle of one sort or another. And the weather ruined it—snow, sleet, or rain. Stubborn rain.

It was nearly dark when we heard the sound of a wagon, its wheels dragging through the mud of the road. I felt such excitement I could hardly contain it. I wanted to leap outside of the confines of the mirror simply to dance my hope of freedom. Surely it would not be long now.

"Mirror?" Ivana's voice cut through my dreams.

"Hurry, to the road," I said. The wagon was nearly past the bend now. And it was heavily laden with goods, obviously a merchant's wagon.

She carried me with her, jolting me with each step. I wished as she went that I had been changed into anything other than a mirror. A cart, a bear, a bird—anything. But the queen had wanted me to know that she could destroy me whenever she would, as she had destroyed the boy, and so many others. It was as much joy as ever she felt, when she knew that she had power over another and could watch them feel it too.

"Help!" cried Ivana. Her voice reverberated from her bones to my glass.

The wagon did not stop. It had passed us by, in fact.

I felt my excitement fade to numbness. I thought of asking Ivana to throw me to the road, to let me be crushed under the wheels of the next wagon. Ivana could go on with her life then. She would be happier in a village no doubt. She would not have to stretch herself then.

But Ivana did not give up as easily as I had. "Help me, please!" she cried again. She ran forward and shrieked her plea again and again.

Suddenly the wagon stopped. It was ahead of us by several wagon lengths, but I could see a female figure on the front, standing and pointing backward. It was the man at her side who stepped out, his embroidered wool coat swirling around him as he moved toward us. His boots were crusted with mud at the bottom but shone with oiling at the top. Good boots, well used.

Ivana stumbled forward. "Please," she said, panting. "Please, sir. Help me."

"Who are you? Why did you call out to me?" the man demanded harshly. His eyes were brighter than I might have wished. It was so much easier to fool those who did not look closely at the details, but I did not know if Ivana would be willing to wait for another.

"My name is Ivana, sir. My fath—" Ivana's voice choked. "My father was killed by bandits." She turned and pointed into the forest. "I narrowly escaped them and returned to the road. Yours was the first wagon I saw."

She was good at this. I had not known she could pretend so well.

"You expect me to believe that tale?" The merchant's face was red with anger. His thick, hairy hands were stiff at his sides.

Ivana's mouth fell open.

Then the figure that had pointed back to Ivana came down from the wagon and stood next to the man. Her face was not at all like Ivana's in shape or coloring, but she was nearly the same height, and her hair was the same wavy, light brown. Her shoulders were also narrow like Ivana's, and her body thin despite her affluence.

But when the girl spoke, it was with a strong, confident voice far different from what I had expected. "Stop that, Father. Can't you see the poor girl is terrified? I think she has suffered enough for one day. Help her get into the wagon and we will all be to the inn that much more quickly."

Ivana was even more astonished at the conversation than I. This was nothing like the relationship between father and daughter Ivana had known.

"We know nothing about her. She could be a bandit herself," said the merchant, gesticulating wildly, his voice so loud it hurt my glass.

But the girl did not seem bothered by it. "A bandit? Her?" she scoffed.

"She could be here to delay us, as the others gather."

"If she is here to delay us, she has already done so,

Father. Where are the bandits she is with?" The merchant's daughter waved her hand into the woods, where there were obviously no bandits waiting.

"I swear, I am no bandit," said Ivana.

"And why should we believe anything you say?" the merchant asked gruffly, though I thought with a little less power in it than before.

Ivana had no answer.

"You should believe her because she has no reason to lie, Father," said the daughter. "Now let her in before she catches her death of cold."

I could see from the twist of his lips that the merchant was wavering.

"You know what Mother would have said, if she were here."

"Your mother died before you were old enough to have any memories of her," said the merchant.

"Yes, she did. But you are always telling me what she was like, and that I am just like her. Tell me truly that my mother would have let you drive by this girl without helping her at least to the next village where she could find shelter, and the chance to contact her next of kin."

The merchant grumbled at this, but he did not deny the truth. "Well, come on," he said, at last, and offered his arm to Ivana.

I was in her other arm, still facing outward as I had

asked her from the first. I could see the quality in the horses as we came close to them. They were a well-matched pair, both black and a similarly terrifying size.

The merchant's daughter had already climbed back into her place. She sat with her arms folded across her chest. Almost, I thought, like a queen. Well, I supposed she was a kind of queen. The queen of her father and all he owned. For a few more hours, at least.

"Your name?" the little queen asked Ivana.

Ivana struggled to answer even as she climbed aboard the wagon. "Iv—Ivana."

"My name is Talia," was the response.

Ivana nodded. "Talia," she echoed.

The merchant caught a glimpse of my glass in the moonlight when he moved to the side. He reached up and brushed against cold glass. "Eh? What's that you've got there?"

Ivana trembled. "A mirror—" she said. Then, haltingly, she added, "It was my mother's. The only thing I have left from her—now."

"Papa," Talia scolded. "You've upset her again. Why don't you just get in and start the wagon forward once more?"

I examined Talia's face more closely from my position at her side. She was rather plain, though she had an interesting face. There was an asymmetry about the cheeks, one higher than the other, but it should not be more difficult to change or to make than any other face.

"It is a fine mirror," said Talia, leaning closer to me. "I am sorry for your loss." She sighed. "I know how it is to be without a mother."

Her father sighed next to her.

"Though now you are without a father, as well. Poor thing."

The merchant sniffed at this but did not argue. He lifted the reins and urged the horses onward.

"Well, no more about what we have lost. Let us think about what we have gained." Talia tucked a hand around Ivana. "I have gained you and you have gained me—and my father, though he may not seem much of a prize at the moment." She laughed lightly at her joke.

Her father held himself stiffly and kept the horses going.

Ivana simply lowered her head. "You are kind," she said.

The two girls rode the rest of the way linked together arm in arm. It seemed that Ivana had forgotten about me entirely. Well, why should I be surprised? I had been forgotten before. It had not stopped me then, and it would not stop me now. Not until I had what I wanted—and was again what I should always have been.

Chapter Four

THE WEATHERED building the merchant stopped at was little more inviting than the stable that stood next to it. If there was magic anywhere near, I did not sense it. Likely I would not want to, if I could.

"Too bad it's the only place near," said the merchant. "The stink's so bad you can hardly tell what the food tastes like. And it's likely better that way."

He left the horses tied outside and escorted Talia and Ivana inside. The inn appeared empty and the fire sputtered close to death. The merchant shook his head, then bellowed, "Woman!"

Talia shrugged at Ivana. "The rooms are large, at least."

Another bellow, this time loud enough to shake my glass: "Woman!"

A red-haired woman with freckled skin appeared by the kitchen door. Her breasts were ripely sized, and she was not afraid to display them openly. I had thought the queen was vain, but this woman was at least as bad, and without reason for it.

"A night's lodging," said the merchant.

"Merchant Minitz," said the woman. She put her hand out for money.

Reluctantly, the merchant put two copper pieces into her hand.

She shook her head and pointed at Ivana.

"Don't take any more room with three than with two," he muttered. But he offered another coin.

The woman offered no thanks. "Stew's over here, if you want some." She gestured to an unsteady wooden table near the hearth.

"What's in it?" asked Merchant Minitz suspiciously. His great cloak had fallen back, and I could see the rounded stomach above his trousers. He was not quite the giant he had first appeared to be, though he had a large head and a long, sharp nose.

"What I had," said the woman, turning her back on him and returning to the kitchen.

Talia and Ivana sat, and Minitz ladled the stew into their bowls. No steam rose from it, and the color was faintly green.

Talia wrinkled her nose. "We have our own food, don't we, Father?"

"A little dried meat for the road," he said. But from the

looks of him, I did not think that would content him. He was a man who loved good food.

Ivana, on the other hand, was content with anything remotely edible. She stared at the stew with ravenous eyes, did not even look for a spoon. She lifted the bowl straight to her mouth and gulped it down.

I cringed at the sight. It was not the behavior of a well-trained merchant's daughter.

Minitz stared and said something under his breath I did not catch. But Talia was more sympathetic. "Oh, I did not realize you were so hungry. I should have thought of it in the wagon," she said.

"Mmmm, mmmm," said Ivana, unaware of the impression she was giving. "Good."

The woman came out for long enough to hear Ivana's praise. "Well, I see one of your kind appreciates a good cook." She went back into the kitchen and brought out some fresh bread of far better quality than the stew. It was only enough for Ivana, however.

She devoured it like a wolf, using it to scrape the gravy from her bowl.

I watched as Ivana finished the last crumbs of bread, which she picked up with a moistened finger from the table. Not, small favor, from the floor. She looked around for something else. Her eyes seemed scarcely less eager for food than before.

Minitz pushed his bowl toward Ivana. "Have mine. I'm sure you'll enjoy it more than I."

Ivana bowed her head and pulled it closer to her. She did think to say "thank you" with her mouth full.

The merchant nodded and said, "You're welcome." I thought I saw a glimmer of real feeling in him. Perhaps he had once been this hungry as well. At least I hoped that he would put it down to hunger alone. Obviously my plan had more flaws in it than I had admitted to Ivana, but this was my chance, and I would hold to it while I could.

"Shall we find our room now?" asked Talia, standing when Ivana was finished eating.

"I'll see to the horse and the wagon." Minitz went out the door, his cloak on again. I wondered how he managed the trick of changing his size with clothing alone. There was no magic in it, yet it worked well.

Talia showed the way to the rickety stairs and Ivana followed, licking at the corners of her mouth where the last of the stew hid.

Talia stopped before the fourth room to the right. "This is the only room Father will ever let us take," she explained. "That's why the woman charges so much."

Inside, there were two straw mattresses on the floor. If I were Ivana, I would have declined either. They were probably so vermin-infested, the wood slats would be more comfortable. I could just see a corner of the ceiling above us. It creaked loudly, and I feared for the roof.

On the other hand, it was large. A dozen merchants and their daughters might have fit inside. And if the window was hand-sized, at least you could see out onto the street, where there were a few torches with enough light to break the pall of darkness.

"I'll sleep here," said Talia, pointing to the mattress in the outside corner, the farthest from the door and the quietest. She was already taking off her gown. The shift underneath was plain, but clean. Ivana had nothing like it.

"I'll sleep here, then," said Ivana, pointing to the bare floor near the door. It was where the room was warmest. And what did she care about noise?

But Talia shook her head. "Take the mattress," she said with a smile.

Ivana was frozen with indecision.

"Father will not sleep on it anyway," insisted Talia. "He likes to be by the door. To protect me—us, now."

So Ivana shrugged and moved to the mattress some feet from Talia. Without stripping, she curled up, tucked me under her head, and began to snore.

Talia had to wake her to offer a thick wool cloak. Ivana took it gladly, and resumed her position on top of me. My view of the world was thus restricted so that I could only hear the thumps of Talia's movements as she prepared to sleep.

"Father will want to take you back to someone," came Talia's voice, after a moment. "There must be an aunt, an uncle. A grandparent—"

Ivana turned to the side, by some miracle still awake. "There is no one," she said.

A brief silence then, though it didn't last for long.

"Oh. Forgive me," said Talia, though she sounded more curious than sorry. "I should not have spoken of it. Father says I'm like a bird singing. I like to hear my own voice speak, even if it doesn't have anything to say. Ah, well. You must think all my questions impolite. I will be quiet now. I promise I will." She clapped small, white hands over pale lips. But they did not stay long. "Oh, but you never told me what town you were from."

I should have thought of this question and prepared Ivana for it. There were so many things I should have done, but I had been absent from the human world for too long. Even when the queen had been with me, she kept me from other people. Now I had forgotten how to predict them and had assumed the queen's habit of ignoring the details. She had had magic to gloss them over, however. I did not.

Ivana looked down at me, her blue eyes begging for help. I told myself it was best I not say anything, even in a whisper. I dared not give myself away.

"I never lived anywhere long enough to think of it

as home," said Ivana at last. Her shoulders fell.

"How sad." Talia sighed. But she did not ask anything further. There was a small pause, and then she said in that birdlike voice, "I will sleep now. I will. Good night."

"Good night," said Ivana.

I waited until after I heard the sound of Talia's even breathing from beneath the window. Then I listened to the sounds below our room. Minitz might not like the woman who owned the inn, but I could hear the roaring sound of his voice shaking the boards beneath us. How many ales had he had? I hoped he would drink himself into a stupor. I needed the time before he interrupted.

"Ivana," I whispered.

A hand moved from her chest to her face. She turned over, leaving me at her back.

"Ivana," I said more loudly. "Wake up."

She started. "Father?" She looked to the left and then to the right, only gradually remembering where she was.

Then her hand moved to find me and lifted me to her face. "Mirror?"

"It is time," I said.

"Time for what?" She was clutching Talia's borrowed cloak tightly.

"For the change."

"Now? But we're safe here, aren't we? Isn't that why you brought me to them?" She stared at the girl across the room.

"Ivana." I made it very simple again. "I will make your face into hers," I said.

"Into Talia's? Why? Her face is not handsomer than mine." Ivana fingered her finely drawn nose, the stretch of skin on her cheeks. It was the first bit of vanity I had noticed in her, and I admit that I enjoyed the thought that for once, I would not be making a face more beautiful.

"It is not a matter of beauty," I said. "But of station. She is a merchant's daughter with a wealthy father, a home—everything you wish for. What will you be if you keep your own face?"

"But the bandits? My story?" asked Ivana.

"Will only last as long as it takes for the merchant to write a few letters. Don't forget his first impression of you. He is not a trusting man."

Yet still Ivana argued. She did not want to give up her face, I suppose.

"But even if you change me to look like her, he will only have to ask a few questions to know who is his true daughter. If there are two of us, he will have to ask."

I had already thought of this. "There will not be two of you, Ivana. You see, I will change her to look like you. Now focus on my glass."

She did as I asked, though doubt twisted her smooth features. I worked around that, changing Ivana's nose into the sharper angle of Talia's. Her mouth turned pale pink, as well, and her eyes were soon speckled with Talia's green and brown.

"There," I said at last. I thanked my luck that I did not have to do the hair strand by strand. I felt weak and thin already, and I would lose yet more magic before the night was done.

"Oh. How strange," said Ivana, touching her face. Should I call her Ivana still? Or Talia now?

I thought of how the queen had refused me my name once I had become a mirror, and I knew I would not do the same to Ivana.

It was then that I remembered Ivana's hands. Thick, hardened, the fingernails broken and dirty, the palms calloused by work. They had passed the brief inspection in the dim light of evening, with the story of the bandits, but they could never be the hands of a merchant's daughter with a doting father.

"A moment," I said, for I had to change those as well.

It was like draining a vessel of water, feeling it grow lighter and lighter in your hands. Except that I was both the vessel being drained and the hands draining. I felt my glass tremble and tried to control it. The image of Ivana's hands shook, and I felt a pain run through me as I concentrated for one more moment, and then another, until the hands were as fitting as the face.

I knew I could not expect thanks from her, but I

wished I did not have to listen to Ivana's complaints.

"But—but—" she got out haltingly. "Will I never have my own face back? Will I have to wear this one forever?"

I did not answer the first question. To the second, I said, "You will wear it until you do not need it any longer."

"And what of her?" Ivana pointed to the other Talia, for there were two of them as yet. "When she wakes, she will complain that she is the real Talia."

She would, of course, do that. But I had thought of this too. If I was to trick the witches who held my magic ahead, I had to practice now. "She will complain that she is the true Talia, but Merchant Minitz will have only to look at her and know that she is mad. He will surely send her away, and then he will have no reason to ask you questions you cannot answer."

Ivana let go of the cloak entirely and left me face up on the floor. I could see her go to the tiny window to look out. "It isn't fair," said Ivana, speaking to me, but looking at Talia's form.

"So?" I argued back. "Do you think everything is fair in life? You think that it is fair your father beat you and Talia's does not? You think it is fair you were born poor and Talia rich?" And was it fair that I had been made a mirror, that my life had been stolen from me by one I trusted and loved? Was it fair I had to live a hundred years on a crumbling wall until a spark of hope arrived for me?

"But she has been so kind to me," said Ivana, biting at her lip.

"You think she has been kind," I said. "But would she have been kind if she knew who you truly were? Would she have been kind to a peasant's daughter who had run from her father with a magic mirror to help her?"

"I don't know," Ivana admitted.

"She is only kind to you because she has plans for you," I said. Hadn't I learned this in my years with the queen? "She will use you in one way or another, if you let her. Now take me to her so that I can finish this night's work."

I thought suddenly of a beautiful woman whose face my sister had taken to attract the notice of yet another nobleman, in her quest to trap the king. The woman had been brought by a man in my sister's employ, who was dispatched with a knife as he turned to leave. The queen was very good with a knife, and I could still hear the sound of the woman's terrified screaming at the sight of so much of the man's blood. Her voice was cut off abruptly, however, as the queen's magic put her to sleep. Then I was held close to the face, to memorize the details.

"Are you ready?" my sister asked.

I was ready, and I did not hesitate. Though I knew

what would happen to the woman once I was done using her face as a guide, I still hoped that my sister would one day remember her love for me and set me free.

Was I any better than my sister when it came to my plan for magic? Well, Talia would be still alive when this morning was done. Whether she would live long after that I could only guess. But her blood would not be on my hands. I could say that for myself, at least.

"Take me to her!" I commanded Ivana, leaving no room for refusal.

Ivana came, her feet moving like lead. She picked me up, carried me step by heavy step to Talia.

"I must see the whole of her face in my glass," I said.

Talia did not even stir as Ivana positioned me. She must feel very secure with her father, for her eyes were fully closed and her breathing came in an even pattern.

I thought again how lucky I was. My half-formed, half-magicked plan was working as well as any the queen had made with years of thought and as much magic to aid her. And soon the real danger to me would be over. With Ivana safely made a wealthy merchant's daughter, it should be simplicity itself to get what magic I needed.

Ivana began to speak, but whatever she said I did not hear her. I was focused on the task at hand, my last great obstacle. I had to strain to make Talia as beautiful as Ivana had been, for my magic was much thinner now.

Then, before I realized it, the merchant's heavy footsteps were coming down the hall. I had forgotten to worry about his arrival.

"Mirror?" said Ivana, breathless. "Mirror?"

"Nearly done, nearly done," I said. Would she become hysterical now and ruin everything? But I had not time to offer calming words. I had become a barrel of honey, and the last part of my magic was too thick to pour. I had to wait for it to come drip by drip.

I finished only a moment before the handle of the door rose, and the hinges creaked. The real Talia's new blue eyes opened slightly, then glazed back over. With a snuffle, she turned so that she faced the wall.

Ivana grabbed me and slid back to her own place, flinging the cloak over her head.

Minitz was too exhausted to notice the flurry. He made a low groaning sound, then bent over and flung off his boots. They landed by us, but luckily, I was not hit.

There was a sigh and the floor creaked with new weight. After a moment or two, there was more heavy breathing.

Chapter Five

AS THE NIGHT fell silent, I imagined what it might have been like if I had once had the courage to make the queen uglier instead of more beautiful. I could have made her into another version of old Zerba. It was what she should have looked like: a haggard witch with a bulbous nose and warts on her cheeks, a hunched back and misshapen legs.

But she would certainly have stopped me before I had finished even her nose. And then she would have taken her revenge on me. Shattered me. Or stolen my life once more, to be placed in a more terrible object. One that had neither voice nor eyes, nor even a mind to think. After all, there were worse things than death. And the queen had had years to refine her abilities to inflict all of them.

"Mirror?" asked Ivana suddenly, interrupting my morbid thoughts.

"Shhh." I had thought she was asleep again. She had lain still all this time.

"Her gown—my gown—"

I groaned.

"Can you use your magic for that?"

"At dawn," I said. "You will take her gown then." There was nothing that could be done about the undershift. Hopefully the merchant would not notice such a detail.

"Without magic?" asked Ivana.

"Not everything is best done by magic," I said irritably.

The queen had taken pride in that, in fact. Of course, she killed on her own, to get magic, and to keep it. But when she might have used a love spell to force the king's feelings, she never did. She whispered into his ear and tickled him with her warm breath. She laughed at the sorriest of his jokes and brushed across his knee with a firm hand. I remember how she told me every detail, since I was not with her to see it for myself.

"If I depended on magic wholly," she had said to me, "I would think less of myself. And no doubt, you would, too, little mirror." As though she cared what my opinion of her was.

But Ivana did care about my opinion. Ivana needed me, or thought she did, as much as I needed her. And so

I told her to sleep for now, to wait for the morning to worry about the rest.

"Sleep? How?"

"With your eyes closed," I answered simply.

She tried, for a time. In the middle of the night, she lifted me to her face and said nothing, only looked at me. After a minute, I felt my glass grow damp, as if my worries had been turned to perspiration.

But no, it was Ivana's tears drowning me.

"Why are you weeping?"

She shook her head, too distraught to speak.

"Is it for your father?"

She shook her head, and pointed to Talia.

"Why are you weeping for her?" I demanded.

"I have never had a friend," said Ivana pitifully.

"A friend!" It was all I could do not to shout the word back at her. "She would never have been your friend," I said. Didn't she see that already?

"But what if she had?"

I would have torn at my hair if I could. Instead, I spoke firmly. "I know her through her face, and I swear to you, she is not worth your tears."

Ivana did not seem to believe me, though. She was so starved for love, I suppose she would seek it out wherever she turned. And I could not tell her it was useless. She would have to discover it for herself. Eventually she would see that love was only a pale version of magic. Magic was the true power that came from life.

Finally, morning came and the sun unfolded pink as a rose. It was a much better light than the one in the night. I was half afraid when I looked at Ivana that I would find I had made some terrible mistake in her looks that I would not have magic enough to fix.

"Ivana?" I whispered.

She turned to me, dark smudges under her eyes. But otherwise, I had done well. She looked the very image of Talia, the merchant's daughter wealthy enough to buy magic to transform me.

"You must trade gowns now," I reminded her.

She did not acknowledge my words. I suppose she had been thinking about it all night and did not appreciate another reminder. She worked slowly.

First, she got out from under the cloak, folded it neatly, and put it to the side. Despite the sunlight, it was not warm in the room and so she shivered as she stripped herself of her dirty clothing. It was then I saw the scars on her back. The similarity between the two girls' figures had made me overconfident. I had not bothered to look for anything else. Well, it was too late for me to change them now. I had to hope that no one would see them.

Bundling up her old gown, Ivana slipped to the corner where Talia lay. Ivana leaned forward to pick up the finer gown, an endless moment when I was sure I should have stayed on the wall and left all things human to those who were human still. For surely there was no chance that this would really work. It was too outrageous, too dependent on chance. And this was only the beginning.

Then Ivana had the gown in her arms and was moving back to me. Miraculously, it had gone as planned. Better than planned, since I had not thought of this wrinkle at all. She held the gown to her face and sniffed deeply, as though the smell were more important than anything else. Then she slid it over her head. The fastenings in back were nearly too much for her stiff fingers, but she managed at last.

"Mirror," she murmured, throwing herself onto the floor beside me.

"You have done well, Ivana. I would hardly think you were new to magic, the way you have taken to it." The praise came easily to my mind, for I was used to the words the queen had used so often with her minions. And with me.

"You did well, Mirror," the queen would tell me. "You know a face inside and out, the bones, the folds of skin, the pores, the shades that make all the difference in the world."

I remembered how I had swelled inside my glass at the sound of her words, thinking that if I did even better the next time, she would release me. A mirror was one thing, but surely a sister was much better.

Ha! She had only been paying me in the cheapest coin she had. And I used it with Ivana, as well. I could certainly not afford to pay her with anything else.

Ivana did not seem as easily appeased as I had been, however. She knelt before me, her hands clasped together as if in prayer. "Even my father would not have done this," she whispered. "He knew the difference between an enemy and a friend."

"Your father knew the difference between friends and enemies," I argued back. "But which did he treat better?"

"His—" Ivana began.

I spoke harshly, twisting words as I twisted faces. "He never touched his enemies as he touched you, I'd wager. He knew that they would touch him back."

Ivana turned away from me.

"Do I not speak true?" I demanded.

"True," Ivana admitted at last. She did not look at me, but she picked me up and went back to her place tucked in her cloak, with me at her side.

In a little while, the occupants of nearby rooms began to stir. Heavy boots clomped down the stairs. A warmth began to spread upward from a new fire in the kitchen, and soon there were scents as well. Fresh bread and a fragrant tea. Sausages.

"Mmm." Merchant Minitz turned over on the floor,

enough for a small figure to get by him—if she were silent enough.

But Ivana kept herself rigid.

"Are you hungry?" I whispered, thinking to get her mind on another topic.

"No," she said stubbornly. But the constant licking of her lips belied her words.

"You should go down and find some breakfast to bring up to your father and your new friend," I urged.

"My father?" She stared around, as though expecting to see the man who had beat her. Her hands went up to protect her new-healed nose. A breath, and she relaxed, her eyes flickering toward Merchant Minitz. "Oh. Him."

"Yes, him," I said. "He is your father now, and you must not forget it."

"My father," Ivana tried out the word.

"Yes. And knowing how he hates the woman of the inn, a loving daughter would help him avoid her." She did not move. "You, Ivana. You are his loving daughter now. Show him."

Ivana got up reluctantly and moved to the door. She turned there and found Talia's boots, still on the other side of the room. With a swift breath, she put them on and went down the stairs.

At the sound of the latch catching, Talia sat up and rubbed at her eyes. It terrified me. Had she been awake before? Had she heard any part of my conversation with Ivana? Did she know what had happened the night before?

I struggled with panic and told myself all the things I had told Ivana. That the merchant would not believe his daughter when she wore another face, that he would be eager to send away the beggar when Ivana agreed to it. But I was not sure I believed it. I had never been as good at intrigues as the queen had been. In truth, I had never used magic for myself at all.

So I trembled when Talia moved closer to me and picked me up, a curious expression on her face. She did not lift me to her face immediately but smoothed her fingers along the lines of my wood. It was as if she did not want to look at what she would see in my glass, and yet she could not help herself. What did she expect to see?

At last, she raised me and her eyes at the same time. There was a silent jolt that I felt press through my wood. Her eyes grew huge, then she put me down, shaking her head. So, it was a surprise to her after all. That was good. It would take her that much longer to recover from it, if indeed she could. By that time Ivana, who had had all night to force herself into her new role—not to mention my careful and experienced advice—would have left her behind long ago.

But Talia had more mettle than I thought. Though her

hands were shaking, she raised me a second time to her face and stared into the new features. I could see her hand slide over each one. The new lips, redder and fuller than before. The new cheeks, new eyes, new nose, new forehead. All an improvement over what she had had before, and she seemed to realize this even as she trembled at the loss of her old self.

"Magic," she whispered at last. But she seemed not to understand it was my magic. She looked to the door through which Ivana had gone. Did she think Ivana had the wits to gain so much magic on her own? Ridiculous.

Then her eyes turned to her father. I could see a tear drop from one, but she dashed away any others and shook her head, as though to refuse sadness. "No. This is not the way I would have chosen to make my place, but perhaps it will be easier, after all. For him, as well as for me."

Why she was berating herself I had no idea. I could only guess that something had gone wrong in what seemed a typical, spoiled merchant's daughter's life and that she had decided that a new face would allow her to change it.

She looked at herself a third time, this time with more unalloyed pleasure than before. She sighed, then nodded. "Yes. I am beautiful. Beautiful enough even for him." She put me down. "And I won't have to give up Father, if I am careful. She can be the daughter who does her duty. I can be the daughter who has what she wants."

Still in her own shift, her eyes narrow and determined, Talia dressed in Ivana's gown, then went over to her father and kissed him while he slept.

"Talia," he said, knowing her in his sleep.

"Good-bye, Father," she said as she stepped away from him. "I love you still."

Chapter Six

IN A FEW minutes came the sound of Ivana's footsteps in the hallway, clumsy with the weight of the tray she was carrying in one hand.

"Father?" she asked shyly, standing in the doorway. Her voice was like Talia's, for that was part of the magic of transforming a face. When the bones were changed, the sound was changed also. But the cadences in Ivana's voice were still her own, mixed with the quavering of her fear.

Merchant Minitz seemed not to notice any difference, however. "What?" he snorted and pulled himself upright.

"I brought you breakfast," said Ivana.

"Ah. That was kind of you. Thank you," said Minitz.

"Of course, Father. I know how you dislike that woman."

"Dislike? Ha! The word is not nearly sufficient to describe my feelings."

"The breakfast smells good, at least."

"Humph. Then she must not have cooked it."

I heard the clatter of silverware against a heavy china plate. Minitz tucked a huge napkin into the neck of his shirt, big enough to cover the whole of his stomach. Then he took a cautious bite of eggs.

He grunted, and took another, larger bite. "No, she definitely did not cook this," he said.

Ivana stared over at the tray, her never-ending hunger rising to her eyes.

Minitz saw it too. "You look as starved as that poor girl last night. Did you not have your fill in the kitchen?"

"No. I did not think of it." Ivana's real father had taught her never to think of herself first. Well, that would change, in time.

"Eat, eat!" the merchant said, waving a hand to the tray. "I can tell you won't be yourself until you've had some food in you."

Had he noticed something after all?

The silverware clanked against the plate again as the food changed hands, and then there was a sound from the corner, from the real Talia. Obviously expecting the confrontation I had warned her about, Ivana started in terror and tipped the tray to one side.

"I am so sorry. I was clumsy," said Ivana, staring at the milk she'd spilled. "I should have been more careful." Her head was down, but she did not try to avoid the blows she thought would come.

Minitz merely stood and shook off a stream of white liquid. "'Tis only milk, Talia. No need to worry."

Ivana seemed astonished that she would receive no punishment.

"Now, do not pretend to be afraid of me," said Minitz, half scolding. "You know that I have tried to give you enough love for a mother and father both. There is only the one matter that we cannot agree on, and that is surely a small thing."

Ivana, bewildered, said nothing.

"What? No argument today? Good, then I will assume you have decided at last that you should trust my judgment."

"I—I—yes," stuttered Ivana. "Of course."

Minitz put his arm around Ivana and patted her back. "Now tell me I have not been too harsh," he said. "Tell me I am a good father all these years."

"You are a good father." There was real feeling in Ivana's voice as she said it. "A wonderful father," she went on, enthused.

Minitz smiled over Ivana's back at this, and I thought how rare a thing a father like this was. I felt a moment's envy before I remembered how little love could be trusted.

"Well, have we left enough for the girl from the road?"

asked Minitz, coming away from the embrace.

White-faced, Ivana moved toward Talia, holding out the remains of the food tray. I wished I had had a chance to tell Ivana what had happened while she was gone.

Talia sat up without a word and ate sparingly. It was strange for me to see Ivana's mouth open so narrowly, her lips so gently blotted. I wondered again what would become of Talia now. Perhaps I was becoming like Ivana, then, with scruples about using another's fate to change my own? So many years with the queen, and yet in only a few days Ivana had made me think the world a place different from any I had ever known.

The silence in the room was broken by the sound of Merchant Minitz stomping into his boots and wrapping himself in his cloak. He took a moment to stare out at the clear day. "Are we ready, then? You know I am always glad to leave this inn."

"Yes, Father," said Ivana.

"Yes, F—" began Talia. But she cut herself off before she gave herself—and us—away.

"And you," Merchant Minitz said, nodding to Talia. "What shall we do with you? Where is your home?"

"With my father dead, I have no home," said Talia boldly.

"Humph," said Minitz. "There must be some place for you. A nunnery, perhaps."

I wondered what she would say to that. I suspected that being in a nunnery would not further her plans, whatever they were.

But Talia seemed amused. I could see the humor dancing in the sudden brightness of her new blue eyes.

The merchant looked to Ivana. "Well," he said. "What do you say?"

I had no chance to tell Ivana to laugh at him. A wrinkle deepened in her forehead, but her father seemed not to notice her confusion.

"It was your idea that she come with us," he said. "Don't you have a plan of some sort?"

"Umm—" said Ivana.

"Oh, come." The merchant clapped his great hands together. "Enough with your teasing me. You always have a plan. Tell me what it is this time and don't make me guess at it, I beg you."

Talia sang a little song under her breath, wordless but powerful. I do not think the merchant knew how it affected him. He only heard it with half an ear.

"Don't you have any guesses at all?" asked Ivana desperately.

The merchant lifted his trousers to the middle of his stomach. "I suppose you want her to come with us, to begin with."

"Yes, yes," said Ivana, relieved.

"And then?" asked the merchant.

Ivana hesitated for a moment. "I'll tell you in good time, Father," she said at last.

I was glad to see her courage had returned to her. I was beginning to think that she would need it in the future, to deal with Talia. Even I had no idea what she intended with all this. It would have been so much easier if I had only one girl to deal with. What would I do with two?

"Out to the wagon then." The merchant turned briefly to Talia. "We will find some place for you, I suppose." He opened the door, and Ivana and Talia moved through it at the same time, bumping elbows.

The merchant looked back, held out his hand to Ivana. She took it.

"Excuse me," said Talia, letting Ivana pass with a semblance of humility.

Ivana held me close to her side, under her cloak, so I could not see anything until we were all three seated in the wagon once more, Merchant Minitz in the middle with the reins and the two girls crowded together on one side of him. Talia, of course, was on the edge. Ivana was next to her new father.

My satisfaction at this proof of the merchant's accepting Ivana did not last long, however. As we drove out of the village, a group of dirty children ran after the wagon.

As soon as I saw them, I recalled another moment with villagers, long ago in my human days.

It had been just before winter, as the last of the brown leaves lay crisping on the dirt beneath our feet. My sister and I were wandering near the edge of the woods by the village when we saw a group of young peasants playing hide-and-seek. I stared at them for a long time. Was that a face I knew? Was that? I had been so long in the forest with Zerba and my sister and magic that I had half forgotten such simple human things as play.

"Come," said my sister. "We have business." She had told me she was sure there was an ailing mother fox ahead, with a den of cubs squirming around her. We were supposed to get to them before it was too late to harvest their lives in magic, but the longing to join in this fun made all thought of magic fly from my head.

"Let's stay and watch. For just a little while," I suggested.

"Watch? Whatever for? You'll get no magic here." She tugged on my arm, but I would not move. Then she gave up. Shrugging, she moved ahead. "Do what you will," she said.

And I did. I watched until the end of the game, when all had been found. Then I eased my way into the group as the counting began again. I spread with a group of girls who were hiding in an orchard of apple trees. They did not speak to me, but I imagined we were hiding together. I perched myself on the highest branch of the tree and waited as the finding began.

I was so intent on watching that I was caught entirely off guard when the first apple hit my head. It was after harvest, so the apples were heavy and overripe. My head ached at the first impact, and then the smell overtook me as the pungent juice of the apple dripped down my face. The flesh of the apple was caught by my hair and stuck there, despite my attempts to shake it out. Then soon after, two more apples hit my shoulders, making my dress sodden and sticky, my body bruised and my hair a mess of applesauce.

The girls I had thought my friends launched at me from their hiding places among the other trees. I could not see their faces to tell which they were, nor their expressions, to tell if they were angry with me or if this was only part of the game. I decided it must be part of the game and began to throw back at them.

A girl fell from her tree to the ground on my third strike. I had not used magic. It was just a lucky hit, but as soon as the girl was down, there were shouts all around me. The hiding was finished. All the children surrounded the tree where I crouched and began to shake the trunk and the branches until I fell out.

"Witch!" they yelled at me. I cowered, my head in my

hands. But they had finished using objects to hurt me and had turned to words. I felt stripped naked before them and was so damaged I did not think of using magic to fight back.

At last, they chased me back into the woods and I found my way home to Zerba's hut. Zerba set me to helping her make a poultice, but I told her nothing of what had happened. I waited until my sister returned.

"You should have come with me," she said when I had finished the whole of the tale. I could tell by looking at her that she had new magic in her, waiting for use. The fox cubs must have been still alive when she got to them.

"I am sorry," I said. I waited for her to offer to share her magic with me, but she never did.

In the morning I saw what she had used her magic for. She had grown her hair down past her knees. She had never had enough magic to do it all at once before, and so had kept putting it off. If she had shared the foxes with me, she would have had to put it off again.

The villagers chasing the merchant's wagon were as malicious as those who had chased me. They shouted taunts and threw things at the wagon. Some of their grime even hit me, though the worst of it was Talia's. She came out at the other end of the village covered with rotten eggs and fruit, a rock that glanced off one cheek, and several old bones in her lap. Ivana looked better than she smelled, and Merchant Minitz had a rising bone bruise on his upper cheek that must have obscured his vision. But he drove the horses hard, long past the danger.

"Peasants," he swore under his breath. "They've never stopped me before and they won't stop me now. No more than animals, the lot of them."

Ivana heard him and stiffened.

The merchant must have noticed, for he slowed the horses at last and put the reins in one hand. With the other, he patted Ivana's shoulder. "You are too gentle to understand," he said.

"I am not," insisted Ivana with a tight voice far removed from any I had heard Talia use.

Minitz gave her an odd look that made me worry a moment. But the moment passed, and nothing happened. I had to trust that he had not guessed the truth, for if he had, what could I do?

Chapter Seven

SOME MILES from the village, Ivana made up the sleep she had missed at the inn. I slid from her hands to the floor, jostling this way and that with the bouncing of the horses. I sensed that there was magic nearby, and my anticipation heightened. Had we arrived already? How could I wake Ivana and let her know what I needed?

But I soon realized that this was not the magic that had called to me from the first. The sense of this smaller magic rose, then fell. From the fading taste and the direction near the woods, I suspected it was a mere hedge witch. If I had to guess, I would have said she tended to use her magic for flying. There was speed in the air, and an edge of daring. I thought using magic for nothing other than a joy of the moment was a shameful waste. But perhaps the hedge witch would think the same of me. Magic for beauty?

Well, no matter. A hedge witch would not be interested

in selling to me her own source of amusement. And she would likely not have much to begin with. The wagon went over a hillock, and the last of the flying magic died away, pushed out by the sharp scent of the greater magic ahead of me. This was the magic I had smelled from the queen's hideaway, and I could settle for nothing less.

At midmorning we stopped and let the horses graze by the side of the road. Ivana and Talia got out to stretch their legs. Merchant Minitz checked the wagon, then moved closer to the girls.

"I am sorry for what I said before, back in the village," he said. "I did not mean to stir up more pain—Ivana." He had to crease his brow with thought to remember the name.

Talia, playing her part, answered, "The pain will be there, whether or not you stir it."

"Ah, yes. That sounds like something my daughter would say. No wonder she is so taken with you. You have much in common." Merchant Minitz looked at Ivana.

But Ivana shrank from his gaze and stared straight ahead.

I lay in the wagon, listening, but unable to help.

It turned out Talia had things well in hand. In her hand. "You remind me of my father, as well," she said.

Minitz made a sound of surprise. He had straightened himself rather abruptly and was now staring at the girl who had been his daughter. "Oh? And what was your father like?"

All my sense shouted danger at me. What was she doing?

"He was a shrewd bargainer," said Talia. "But he never loved money as much as he loved me."

Minitz laughed, not lightly. "No father could. A daughter is as precious a gift as any man could wish. Eh?"

Nudged, Ivana looked up. "Some men prefer sons," she said.

But Merchant Minitz only laughed heartily. "Ha! Only a fool would trade a daughter for a son."

"My father said much the same thing," Talia put in. There was a long pause afterward, and I felt there was import in it, but I did not understand what. "And yet—" Talia's voice trailed off, wistful and hopeful at once.

"And yet?" Merchant Minitz echoed.

Talia shrugged. "He wished to marry me away. To a man I had never met, but whom my father thought a good match for me."

Ah! So that was it! For the first time I found some sympathy for the girl. How we wished to be free, all in our different ways. Me from my mirror, Ivana from her father, and Talia from a betrothal. Well, magic would serve us where love had not.

Minitz climbed back into the wagon then, and I saw

him motion to the two girls. "Perhaps," he said, putting out a hand to Ivana when she stepped up. "Perhaps a girl such as yourself does not understand what is best. Perhaps she should leave that to her father."

I thought that Talia might continue to argue, but she didn't. We went several miles farther, and the brown and unruly hills were replaced by well-tilled fields, sprouting with a green so bright it might have been magic.

Ivana was stunned by the sudden color. She put a hand to her heart, as if to keep it inside her chest. Then she breathed out, "Oh, how wonderful. I have never seen anything so wonderful."

Merchant Minitz pulled back on his reins, and the horses slowed. "Talia, you've seen it a hundred times before," he said.

Frantic, Ivana's hands pulled at each other, marring the flawless skin I had worked so hard to perfect. "Yes, but—" she stuttered.

"True beauty is just as wonderful the hundredth time as the first," Talia filled in for her.

Minitz looked closely at Ivana, then at Talia. His eyes narrowed, and he tapped at the bridge of his long nose in thought. I felt a thrill of terror run through me. Ivana must have felt the same. But at last, Minitz shook himself, and turned his attention back to the horses.

Why could I not have found a dull merchant, I

thought, one with a daughter who had no plans of her own?

Late that afternoon, the road widened at a shallow marsh and Minitz pulled the horses to the side to allow them to drink.

"Talia, get the basket for lunch," he said, waving at the back.

Ivana hesitated a moment, then turned to the back of the wagon. After searching carefully, she found what she needed. It was perched at the top of the front load, secured with a rope.

Ivana got off the wagon with the basket in her hands, and Talia came after her. I was happy to stay where I was and rest my mind and my worries, though I could not sleep.

After sitting down, Merchant Minitz began to speak. "Ivana," he said, looking at Talia. "Would you tell me the name of the man you were to marry and the city where he lived?"

I expected Talia to hem and haw, but she did not. Her voice was clear and sure as she said, "His name is Peter. Peter Blenin. And he is from Yulov."

"Blenin of Yulov?" echoed Merchant Minitz.

"You know of him?" On the surface her voice was even, but I heard the intensity underneath. It told me at last why she had traded her place in the world for a beautiful face.

She was in love with this man, this Blenin. I could have laughed aloud at my sudden relief. This was her plan? I had thought her like the queen in intelligence and determination. But the queen had known enough not to fall in love.

"I have heard the name," said Minitz. "A well-born man, if I recall. Very handsome, but rather easy with his money." He stood up and began to walk back and forth so that I could see his face. His expression was dark and troubled. "I am surprised that your father would have offered you to him," he said.

"He only needs a good woman to temper him," said Talia, her face flushing. Then she added, "At least, that is what my father used to say."

Had she said too much?

Sitting down, the merchant said, "Ah, well. You could do worse, I suppose. And he was your father's choice."

"Yes." A hint of defiance. Talia lifted her chin. "He was my father's choice."

Obviously he was not her father's choice. And since she had embraced her new face, I suspected he did not know he was her choice, either. Well, what a surprise he would have. I hoped I would be there to see the end of it.

Finally, Merchant Minitz nodded. "I would never stand in the way of a father's plan for his daughter."

"Good," said Talia. But she relaxed her thin shoulders too soon in my opinion.

Be careful, I thought. Always be careful. And when you are offered what you have always dreamed of, be more careful still.

Merchant Minitz warmed to the idea. He clapped his hands. "Yes. I will see to it myself." His voice boomed, but was there a note of falseness in it? But he went on. "Perhaps you shall wed next summer on the same day as"—was I the only one who heard that tiny hesitation?—"my own daughter. Eh? How would you like that, Talia?"

Ivana was not used to her new name, and so it took her a moment to respond. "Wed?" she asked. She must have been thinking of old Vanye, for there was a quaking in her voice.

"Indeed," said Merchant Minitz. "You should show Ivana the letters Duke Fensky has sent you. They prove his worth, do they not?"

"Yes, yes," stammered Ivana. "Of course."

Minitz turned to Talia. "Not that I mean to hint that your father's match is any worse for you, of course."

"Of course," murmured Talia.

"And you are both such dutiful daughters. A father could not hope for more obedience to his wishes." Was I so used to hearing the queen's sarcasm that I heard it where it was not meant?

Ivana bit at her lip and clutched her hands together tightly. With her original complexion, the gesture would not have been so noticeable, but with Talia's pale skin, her knuckles seemed to glow red.

"Your upcoming marriage to the duke does not still trouble you, does it, my daughter?" asked Minitz.

Ivana stared helplessly in my direction. Her mouth opened and closed. Then opened and closed again. Finally, she found something to say. "I feel I hardly know him, Father. That is all."

"She does not know him?" asked Talia, pretending surprise. "Should she not have some choice in the matter of her own marriage?"

Utter silence, which was broken by the sound of excrement falling from one of the horses.

"Well," said Merchant Minitz as he walked, head lowered, toward the wagon. It was not clear to me to which of the girls he spoke. "Your mother and I did not choose each other when we married. In fact, we had never met before the day we were joined together forever. But that did not hinder us from happiness." Minitz harnessed the horses once more, then climbed in back. But he did not start the wagon moving, not yet.

"I trusted my parents," he said, his eyes shifting back and forth between the two girls. "You must trust me as well."

With that, Minitz clucked at the horses, and they

moved toward the rise ahead. When we had crested it, the horses stopped a moment and we looked out over a vista. It showed a nicely sized town stretched out before us, and an overwhelming force of magic somewhere nearby. Even more than I suspected, enough to make me fear it rather than anticipate it eagerly. This was no group of small witches gathered together for mutual protection or profit. This was a single witch, powerful and sharp. Would she have need of anything at all? And could I hope to steal from such a source?

I told myself I would rather make a fruitless try at the magic than not try at all. But the truth was, I had to go forward now. I had set myself on this path, and it moved me along whether I wanted it to or not.

The horses were not as sensible. At the sense of magic, they lifted their heads and took high steps that moved the wagon backward instead of up the road.

The merchant pulled harder on the reins and muttered to himself. "Can't understand what is wrong with them. They've never acted this way before."

So that might mean it was new magic. Good for me. A witch who had recently come to the area might be less sure of herself.

I thought of the rival witch who challenged the queen as she carried me all day through the forest near her hideaway. The rival had been young, but horribly plain.

Obviously, she did not use her magic on herself, as the queen did. She must have assumed this would give her an advantage in battle, for she demanded a duel.

The queen pretended to be reluctant. She asked simply, "Where?"

"Wherever you choose," said the rival with a shrug.

If I had any doubt then as to who would win, it disappeared at this nonchalance. Even the queen was not so arrogant as to give away the advantage of her own ground.

"Here, then," said the queen, waving a hand to the trees around us.

"And what shall we duel with?"

The queen pointed at me.

"A mirror?" The rival was surprised, and pleased. This seemed to further her sense of superiority.

"Do you object?" asked the queen.

"Oh, no. No. You bring your mirror. And I will bring my spectacles." The rival's eyes gleamed darkly in her olive-colored skin.

"Come at dawn," said the queen.

And they were there at dawn, both of them. The rival wore her spectacles proudly, but pride alone would be no help to her.

For a moment, I considered doing nothing in the queen's defense. But the queen's losing this battle would not make me free. Besides, I knew better than to think the queen would trust her life solely to me. She would have something else to save her, and once the rival was dead, she would turn her attention to me.

The queen lifted me. "What would you do?" she asked, staring across the barren garden. It had once been filled with growth, but the queen had taken it over for her experiments and sucked life from even the worms in the dirt. The trees were gnarled and fruitless, the air acrid and still.

"Fill me," I said. "And I will transform the ground beneath her feet to quicksand."

"No, too easy a death," said the queen.

The rival used her spectacles to guide her shaft of burning magic straight to the queen's heart. But the queen turned it aside with a wave of her hand.

"Fill me," I said again. "And I will turn her into a bird, a deer, or a hound."

"Too kind," said the queen.

The rival used her spectacles to guide a cut at the queen's legs. The queen leaped over it and the rival's eyes grew large in her own spectacles. The rival took a step backward. But it was too late for retreat now.

"Be filled," said the queen. And she began to give me a portion of her magic. "And turn her into a tree."

I opened myself to receive the magic, but it was not what I had hoped for. Not nearly enough to make a full transformation. I shot it at the rival, twisting her legs into roots, her arms into branches. But even when I had exhausted the queen's gift, the rival's face remained untouched. Her spectacles, still magical, clung to her face, but she was too terrified to use them a third time.

Looking at her was a glimpse of the only escape I should ever have expected from the queen. I imagined what it would be like to be half a woman, with a face and a torso, but no arms or legs. Or to have arms and legs, and a mirror for a face. It would be something equally horrible, I was sure. For the queen would never let me be whole and apart from her.

The queen walked toward her rival and dashed the spectacles to the ground, smashing them with her heel and sucking their magic into herself as she did so.

"You should not have challenged me," she said, and she prepared to take the rest of the rival's magic, as it flew out of her in death.

The branches of the tree shook. The rival began to beg. "Please. Take my magic, if you wish. But let me live. Please, let me live."

"I will let you live, then," said the queen.

The rival let go her guards against theft, and her magic streamed to the queen. It did not take long. Then the queen turned to her. Perhaps the rival realized at last how foolish she had been to trust the queen's word.

"You promised," she muttered. "You promised."

But the queen only said, "You will live." Then she lifted her hand and the rival's noises stopped as the last bit of humanity disappeared from the form of the tree. Yet it was alive, as nothing else in the garden was.

"I honored my word, did I not?" the queen asked me.

"She is alive," I said.

"In fact, she will live a very long time," said the queen.

"Perhaps," I said, and thought of the immortality the queen had given me when she gave me my form. There were times when mortality was far preferable. If the tree could have spoken, I was sure she would have agreed with me.

The queen then stretched out a hand as if around a piece of fruit. An apple grew into it with magic. And from the smell of it, it held the taste of death. The queen did not pluck it then, however.

"This will be useful another day," she said, and left the apple hanging. In the white and gray of winter, the apple showed bright red.

Chapter Eight

SUDDENLY, THE horses neighed high-pitched and long. It was a terrifying sound. I felt it reverberate in my glass and almost spoke. I wanted to ask Ivana to take me off the floor of the wagon and hold me safe in her lap, but I remembered in time I could not reveal so much of myself.

"Whoa, whoa!" Merchant Minitz held tight to the reins, but the horses were panicked. Minitz swore under his breath. Sweat dripped from his jaw, running in rivulets down his face. "Roe, Frell," he said, calling the horses by name. They seemed to breathe in as one and hold their places.

I thought for that moment that I was safe, that Minitz would keep control. Then the reins, pulled past their strength, broke. The horses bolted, careening off the road, toward the valley below.

Minitz was thrown from his position at the front of the wagon. He had leaned forward to calm the horses, and so it was easy for him to lose his balance and fall to the side. He was not run over by the wheels of the wagon, but other than that I could not tell if he was hurt.

Ivana was next. She screamed as the horses hit a gallop. The wagon hit a rock, and Ivana let go of the side of the wagon. She tumbled head over heels off, landing a few yards distant from the merchant's place. I saw him scramble toward her and help her up. Then Minitz turned his attention to the wagon, and the girl who was left inside it.

"Jump!" he cried. I could not tell if Talia heard him over the mad pace of the horses and the creak of the wagon. "Jump away from the horses!" But Talia did not do it.

I did not have enough magic to change the size of the wagon or make the horses smaller, and neither of those would have saved us from being dashed to our deaths regardless. Instead I prepared myself for the end and hoped that at least this death would be quicker and more complete than the one the queen had given her rival.

Then I saw Talia leaping over me, crossing the chasm between wagon and horse, making a bridge of herself. Her hair flew behind her and small body landed hard, though she made no sound of pain. She moved immediately to put her mouth to the ear of the lead horse, Roe. I do not know what she said, but I could see the change. The horse shivered, its eyes rolling. Then its hooves slowed and it raised its head.

Now only one horse was going wild, but that made things even more dangerous, for the wagon was unbalanced and it was fast approaching the sheer cliff. But Talia acted with perfect aplomb. She took hold of Roe's mane and raised herself to a crouched position on his back. She jumped onto Frell with magnificent grace, then spoke to him as she had to the first horse.

I was sure we would go over anyway, but the wagon stopped just short of the precipice. From my precarious position near Talia's feet, I had a glimpse through a crack in the wagon boards of the rocks below, colored red as blood with the falling sunlight.

Talia was rubbing Frell's great black cheek with her own olive-colored skin when Minitz came running up from behind.

"You idiot!" he shouted, grabbing firm hold of Talia's arm. He shook her once, hard. Then he put his arms around her, as if to make sure she was still alive. He came away from her slowly and kept his grip on her arm. "What did you think you were doing?" he asked in a hoarse whisper.

"Saving your wagon," said Talia, breathlessly. "And your horses."

"Damn the horses," said Minitz. "You could have been killed."

Talia shrugged, though I could see from the line of her shoulders that this was not a trifling matter to her. Not in the least. "My mother is dead," she said. She looked at the merchant and the tension in her back tightened. "My father is dead as well. What did I have to lose?"

It was a real question, and Minitz answered it with fervor. "Never say that. Your father would not want you to die for no reason. Neither would your mother, I am sure. And what of your betrothed?"

There was a pause. Then Talia whispered, "I did not think of him. Strange."

"Is it?" said Minitz, too softly for anyone to hear but me. Then he helped Talia away from the wagon and, step by step, coaxed the horses backward. When they were a safe distance from the cliff, he allowed them to turn and make their way back up the hill. Near the road again, Minitz stopped to get new leather from the back of the wagon and made new reins from it.

Finally, we were on our way again. Still, I could feel the strain of the horses as we moved down the steep path to the valley. The magic that had spooked them—and me—was still there. It was as powerful as it had been when I first tasted it, and I was more sure than ever that it was concentrated in one witch. One very powerful witch. I tried to tell myself it was for the best. Only one witch to seek, only one witch to pay. One witch to fear.

By the time I noticed the wagon again, we had reached the open bowl. The horses had found a regular rhythm again, and Minitz and Talia seemed caught in their own undecipherable thoughts. But Ivana, staring toward the place of her new home, was an open book.

She felt hope and fear at once.

As I did, though for a different reason entirely.

It was growing dim by the time we reached the merchant's house. The sun streamed gold and copper in the sky, and the horses pulled to a halt before a large building. What I noticed first about it was the feel of magic that drifted in wisps through windows and doors. Not great magic, however. Nothing like the new magic the horses had sensed at the top of the hill—and tried so hard to escape.

No, this was ordinary small magic drawn from household pests, and I suspected the cook, simply because I could think of little else to do with such magic other than to improve the flavor of an undercooked bit of bread or a burnt piece of meat. It would hardly be enough for me to turn a mosquito into a butterfly, but I thought I would take it anyway. It would be safe to have, after all, and a good beginning to shore me up against the other, darker source.

But for now I would focus on the rather unmagical

collection of stones in front of me. The merchant's house was no castle with winding turrets and gargoyles. But it was a fine home nonetheless, with lights in the windows that seemed to wink and welcome. I could see that Ivana was overwhelmed by the wonder of it, for it would have bought ten villages the size of the one she had lived in with her father.

Merchant Minitz got out of the wagon and offered Ivana a hand first.

"Thank you," she said and climbed out awkwardly with one hand, concealing me behind her back with the other.

"You're welcome," said Merchant Minitz. Then he walked around to the other side. "It is not your father's home," he said as he helped Talia to the ground, as well. "But perhaps you will find some comfort here." After the incident with the horses, his reaction to her was less hesitant—or more real.

"I cannot imagine a more wonderful home," said Talia. Then she showed her first sign of feeling after a brush with death. "Or a more wonderful father," she added. Bold as ever, she hopped down, straight into the merchant's arms, and gave him a quick kiss on the cheek.

Merchant Minitz held his hand up to his cheek, simply enjoying the moment. Then he cupped his hands to his mouth and boomed: "David! Silva! We're home!"

A door opened, and then another. The house breathed with voices; its heart beat with the flutter of footsteps.

"Sir." A woman with a soft face and a softer body came close enough for me to be certain she was not the practitioner of magic here. She smelled only faintly of it, and only on her clothes. It had not seeped into her hair and skin, as it would have, had she put it to use herself. "We did not expect you for another day. Nothing is ready," she said.

"It is no matter, Silva," said Merchant Minitz. "We are home. We will take it as we left it."

"Home," said Talia softly.

Ivana made no sound but a squeak of surprise as the servant woman embraced her heartily.

"You are a stone," said the woman, with a half-laugh. Then she noticed Talia. "And who is this?" she asked.

"Her name is Ivana," said Minitz, smiling as he took in her wind-blown hair and the sweat shining on her face. In truth, she looked almost as much a peasant as Ivana ever had in the same face. Perhaps it was not so strange, though. The queen had changed too, when she put on a new persona. At least for a time.

"But—?" the woman began.

I think she did not dare to say the rest of it. Who was this person and why was she here?

Minitz answered in his own way. "You are to treat her

as you treat Talia," he said and turned toward the house.

"Yes, sir," said Silva, a moment late.

"And I hope there's food!" Minitz called back to her.

"Yes, sir. Yes, sir," she said, and followed after him. "There's always food for the merchant."

Merchant Minitz led up the steps and into the front room. The fire was well stoked there, and the furnishings in fine condition and good taste. A little on the older side, perhaps, but not worn. The colors were subdued, not what I would have guessed Merchant Minitz or Talia would have chosen. Perhaps his wife, before she had died. The magic was slightly stronger here, as a tea would be, left to steep a few minutes more. The kitchen, definitely, I thought.

"They are so like," muttered Silva. "Even their figures are the same. Which is just as well, for otherwise I would have nothing to put her in until the seamstress came and finished making some new gowns.

"But he said to treat her as Talia. Perhaps that means she is . . ." She trailed off, then shook her head. "No, no. I won't believe it of the master."

I realized that she believed Talia was Merchant Minitz's illegitimate daughter. How long would it be before the house was buzzing with rumor? Not long, I wagered.

Ivana carried me into dinner and I got a good look at

the Minitz's cook. She was a tall woman, and thin, which seemed unusual for a cook. Until I thought of her need for magic, and it made more sense. She knew what she did to the food. Perhaps with the addition of magic, it might taste better. But that did not mean she would eat it with gusto.

The cook wore a voluminous apron and patted at it frequently, as if to check that her supplies were still there. I did not see a knife or spoon emerge, but as the merchant sat beside the cutting table that had been covered with a stained cloth and a few chipped dishes, I twice saw a flash of tiny particles floating through the air. Ivana sneezed once when she came too close to one cloud, but there was no magic in the herbs. The cook thought there was, perhaps, but the magic had been suffused into the apron itself. If she were a real witch, perhaps I would think more about paying her for what I planned to take. But she seemed to only half understand the magic herself. I doubted that she would have the ability to keep me from taking what I wanted or to seek me out afterward.

"Here. Eat well, Master Minitz," said the cook as she brought out a loaf of bread that had not been baked this week, though it smelled fresh and light a moment after it appeared.

"Thank you, Mrs. Franzen. You have such a way with food. I think sometimes that you could bake in the middle of the woods without a fire and still make my mouth water."

Too true, that.

"Are you sure I can't convince you to come with me on one of those long journeys south for goods to sell?"

Talia stiffened at this. Obviously she did not like the cook as well as her father did.

The cook waved her hand and tutted, though from her color she was obviously pleased by the compliment.

"Well, thank you for your work tonight. I'm sorry to keep you up so late. You can clean up after us in the morning." It was a dismissal, and the cook felt it. Her pleasure dissipated. She nodded stiffly and retreated, taking the scent of her magic with her.

She made it easy not to feel sorry that I would soon be stripping her to her bare skills. After all, she would be able to gather more magic eventually. In another year or two, the merchant would like her food again. If she lasted that long in her current position.

Ivana stared at the food laid out and moved toward it slowly. She had learned enough since last time to pick up a fork with one hand. It meant that she could not hold me, however. So she laid me on the floor, tucked between the chair and the leg of the table. It was not a good position for watching, but I could hear all there was to hear.

Merchant Minitz told tales of wrangling with other merchants in the north. Talia laughed heartily. Ivana pretended to do the same. Finally, Minitz drank the last of the wine and his boots made a loud sound on the floor next to me. "To bed, now, you two," he said.

"Oh, must we?" said Talia.

"Yes," said the merchant, with a smile. "You must."

Talia stood. "Good night, then, Fa—" She stopped, a daring look on her face. "May I call you Father?" she asked suddenly.

Minitz took a sharp breath, as if offended.

Talia's face turned pale, though her eyes burned like dark stars in a white sky. "I am sorry. I should not have asked that. It is only that—" Her voice broke.

The merchant reached for her, as if to embrace her again as he had after the danger of the horses was over. Then he pulled back and only stroked her cheek with the back of his hand. "It is no affront to be asked such a thing by you," he said. "A compliment, rather."

"You have made me so happy," chattered Talia. "I thought after my father died that I could never be happy again. But you are so much like him. So good, so kind. . . ." She trailed off at last.

Minitz grunted, then cleared his throat. Stepping away from Talia, he looked back at Ivana. "Would you mind?" he asked.

Ivana's shoulders made the smallest movement of assent.

It was not at all what the real Talia would have done. She would have spoken at length about her thoughts on the matter. But Ivana could no more do that than she could dance a reel in a hall full of partners.

Minitz straightened and faced Talia once more. "You would not think it a betrayal of your own father?" There was great emotion in his voice.

"No," said Talia, almost choking on the word.

Minitz hesitated a moment more, extending Talia's agony. Perhaps she deserved it. But in the end, the merchant could not resist. Talia wearing Ivana's face was as persuasive as she had been wearing her own. She knew well how to manipulate her father and at the same time make him love her for it.

"I would be honored if you would call me Father," said Minitz sincerely. As an afterthought, he added, "And Talia, you have always said you wished for a sister."

"Yes," murmured Ivana. "I have."

How foolish she was, I thought, if she had said such a thing. It was what I had wished once as well, and look what that wish had brought me.

"Well, now you have one," said Merchant Minitz.

Ivana, restless, shifted me from one hand to the other. A flash of light gave me away.

"What is that you are holding there?" asked Merchant Minitz suddenly. He pointed to Ivana's hands—to me. "Ivana's mother's mirror?"

Ivana stood very still, but I could hear the thunderous beat of her heart.

Talia saved her. "I wanted to give it as a gift," she said. "For all Talia has done for me. It is all I had to offer."

"Hmmm," said Minitz. A long pause. Surely he knew. Too many clues, given by both girls. And the horses. And me.

He spoke through thin lips, a flash of—was it anger or a devilish sense of humor?—in his eyes. "I suppose you must accept a well-meant gift graciously, then, Talia."

"Yes, Father," said Ivana.

"Thank you," said Talia.

It was then I was sure that the merchant knew the truth about Ivana and Talia, and me as well. Why he did not say something I could only guess at. He was playing some kind of game, and I would have to play it too. To the end, wherever it took us.

Chapter Nine

IVANA REACHED the stairs, took one step up, then stopped in uncertainty. Talia nearly ran into her from behind. She was not at all unsure but looked back to see if there was anyone watching. There was.

"Too sleepy to remember your own room, Miss Talia?" asked Silva, with a hint of laughter in her voice. She put a gentle hand on Ivana's shoulder and ran her fingers through the hair. I wondered if she had done that since Talia was a child, and if she would notice any difference now. I had not bothered with the hair.

But she said nothing and I could detect no hint of wariness in her voice. "Come, I'll show you and Miss Ivana together." She let go of Ivana and walked ahead.

Following behind Silva, Ivana held me so that I could see the long staircase and the fine paintings of forbearers, as in a noble's house. She stopped a moment before the face of a woman that might have been her new one, except for the age.

"Ah, a fine woman your mother was," said Silva. "I wish many a day she was here with us still. And to see you grown like this—" A long sigh.

After a moment, Silva led down the corridor. "Here you are, Miss Ivana," she said, pointing to a tall, dark door. "Sleep well. I'll send someone in to help you dress in the morning."

Ivana nearly answered her, but Talia spoke first. "That's kind of you, Silva. Thank you."

With a nod, Silva closed the door behind her and led Ivana down the hall to her room.

"Thank you," Ivana said, as Talia had.

"You're welcome, Miss Talia. Call for me if you find yourself worrying over any sounds. Though, knowing you, you will be more likely to search them out yourself and destroy them." She smiled again. It sounded as though she knew Talia quite well. How soon before she noticed the difference in Ivana?

"If you begin sleepwalking, I daresay I'll have to get David and your father both to help you back to your room. There's no waking you while you're in that state, and it will take more strength and courage than I have to confront you." Silva pointed to a scar on her forehead. "That's what I got the last time."

"I'm sorry," said Ivana.

Silva waved her hands. "No, no. I'm happy to have it. I always tell the other servants at the market I got it from the merchant's daughter, and that she is as strong as any son could have been." She went off chuckling to herself.

Ivana stepped inside the room. A single candle was lit on a vanity, before a larger mirror. By its light, I could see the window looking out over the courtyard the wagon had entered, and the hill above. The room was filled with a sumptuously sized bed, and there was a wardrobe by the window, so overflowing with gowns that its door would not close. I guessed that Minitz did not want his daughter, lacking as she was in natural beauty, to lack for anything else.

Ivana sat before the larger mirror and set me to the side. Then she stared at the flickering reflection of her new face. None of her old beauty had made the change to her new face, but all her old doubts of herself were there, clear as ever in her darting eyes and her unsmiling lips. She looked down at her hands, perhaps more satisfied with them.

I wondered if it was time for me to warn her about the merchant's suspicions. No, better to wait for a time when she seemed reluctant to do what I asked of her. For now I would stay with requests that would be easy for her to obey.

There was a knock on the door.

"Come," said Ivana. She stood up.

It was Talia. She lingered in the doorway, as if between two worlds.

"Well?" asked Ivana.

Finally, Talia came in and closed the door behind her. The two stared at each other for a long time. They were cautious of each other, no doubt, because each held the other's secret. I was surprised they were not more antagonistic, but perhaps they had already worked too long together to continue their shared deception.

"I suppose you want to know why I said nothing about this." Talia waved at her face. If I had thought it would look more beautiful with her poise and confidence, it did not. At least not now, as she faced Ivana.

"You are wondering what it is I have to gain in losing my father, my home, my name, and my very face to you. Well, it is simple enough. I love Blenin." She waited for Ivana to make a comment, but she said nothing.

"The duke is a good catch. He has a fine reputation and his letters are well written, but I do not burn for him. Can you understand what that is, to love someone and to know that you cannot have him? No, I can see you do not." Talia sat on the edge of the bed and stared at Ivana.

"Do witches never learn to love?" she asked.

"I am not a witch," said Ivana fervently.

"Oh no?" Swift and smooth as a snake, she reached around Ivana and grabbed at me. "I suppose next you will try to tell me that this is no magic mirror?"

Ivana's mouth opened and closed, but no words came out.

There was no reason for me to pretend. If Talia meant to betray us, she would have done it long ago. "I am a magic mirror," I said. Though that was only part of the truth. "And I have seen enough of the world to wonder about a girl who says a man loves her and who also wishes to change her face."

Talia blushed, and her hands went up as if to warm themselves on her embarrassment. "What does a mirror know of love?" she asked, dismissively.

"What does a girl your age know of love?" I flung back at her. "How old are you? Seventeen? Eighteen?"

"Sixteen," admitted Talia dully.

"Ha!" I said.

But Ivana was all curiosity. "Where did you meet him?" she asked.

Talia, watching her every movement in the large mirror, waved a hand imperiously. "From some business Father had with him." Her eyes glowed, and she moved forward off the bed with lips parted, as if Blenin was in the mirror, waiting for her.

"What is he like?" asked Ivana.

"Handsome," said Talia immediately. "Charming. Beautiful lips. Firm white teeth."

It might have been a horse she was talking of.

"And he has a sense of humor that is very keen, with a laugh you could never be tired of hearing."

"And is he blind, as well? So that he will not notice that you come to him with a new face?" I asked. Perhaps it was cruel, but I had no wish to be kind to her. She had not treated me well, and I determined to make her see me as more than merely a mirror.

Talia shrunk back a bit. She shrugged. "He will not mind a new face," she said.

"Because he does not love you," I said. "Is that not so?"

She hesitated a moment, then flung me back to the vanity. I was lucky I was not damaged, for she showed no care for me. "He did not notice me, that is all," she defended him. "He has an eye for beauty, and what it wrong with that?"

"What does your father think of him, though?" asked Ivana. Of course, the merchant's opinion would matter to her above all else.

"He will see Peter in his true light," said Talia. "But it will take time."

"You mean he does not think of this Blenin well now. Why is that, pray tell?" I said.

Talia spoke reluctantly. "Because on the day of our meeting, my father had a note of credit from Peter, bought from someone else. Father took it to Peter to be redeemed."

It was not hard to guess the rest. "It was not redeemed," I said.

Again, Talia jumped to the man's defense. "He does not have money lying about. He uses it, in investments. He is waiting for a good bit to return to him larger than before. Then he will pay Father back what he owes, and more."

Was this what he had said or only what she had made up for him? "Of course," I said.

"He will pay him," she insisted. "Likely when Father sends him the note about our betrothal. He will come here and see me. Then he will give Father the money."

"And marry you." Clever as she was, Talia told a simple story in her head. One where no one acted but in the ways she demanded.

"I think we shall be very happy, Blenin and I," said Talia. She looked at herself in the large mirror again, and any of the doubts that my questions had seeded in her were blown away in her certainty. She looked like a girl who stared out at a distant scene in a painting, one that showed no detail and for that reason, no mistakes, either.

"But what of Duke Fensky? Your father will expect me to marry him now, and I know nothing of him," said Ivana.

I did not blame her for changing the subject. Who wanted to listen to Talia enthuse over a man who sounded more mythical than real? If she and he were as happy as she expected, I would turn them both into eternal lovebirds, so that they might sing of each other forever. I much doubted it, however.

"I do not know him, either, except through his letters," said Talia. "And while the duke writes well enough, there is something hidden in his words, as if it is too dark to be admitted."

I did not know whether Talia's opinion on the matter could be trusted or not. Considering her view of Blenin, I should make sure Ivana was cautious. There was no way of knowing if Talia was too kind to the duke or too harsh with him.

"Still, I could not think of a way out of marrying him without hurting Father and making myself look a fool. A duke for a merchant's daughter? Impossible to refuse."

"But what is his reason for wishing to marry you?" I asked. "If he has never met you, it cannot be that he was overwhelmed with your beauty."

The sting touched Talia only briefly, and when she looked in the mirror again, she saw what she had become. Instead, it was Ivana whom I hurt, all unwittingly. You see how long it had been since I was last among humans? There are certain things that come slowly, if at all.

"Is it your father's wealth?" I asked.

"Hardly," said Talia. "Father is wealthy by our standards, but the duke has his own estates, and he is known far and wide as a man who uses his means well."

Well, perhaps that was good for Ivana. But perhaps it was not. The truth was, I could think of no reason a duke with his own means would lower his sights to a merchant's daughter. Especially one who looked like Talia had, and Ivana did now. Was there something wrong with the man?

"Letters," said Ivana suddenly. "The letters from Duke Fensky your father said you had—?"

"You want me to get them? You may have them and good riddance. Whenever I see them, I feel uneasy." Talia moved to the wardrobe that had been hers. On the top shelf was a sheaf of papers. She brought them down and placed them in Ivana's hands.

Ivana stared at them. I looked too, admiring the careful form of the writing. A man with something to hide, indeed. "Has your father ever met the duke in person?" I asked suddenly.

"Briefly," said Talia. "But it was in the dark, at night. The duke was on a horse and came by as Father was trying to cross a river. The duke offered him a ride across and Father took it."

"And he decided he wished to marry you because of your father?" I asked skeptically.

Talia shrugged. "Because Father told him about me."

"What did he say?" What could he possibly have said?

"That I had a good heart and a fiery spirit," said Talia.

"Father said I was like my mother, and that if only she had lived, he would have been the happiest of men. Father can be enthusiastic when he talks about Mother."

We all knew that, from the wagon ride.

"He also told Duke Fensky that he had always believed arranged marriages were best, that parents made better decisions about their children's spouses than ever a child could alone." There was resentment in Talia's tone now, the warmth when she had spoken of her father and mother long cold. "He even told Duke Fensky that it was often better if the marriage were made blindly, sight unseen. It embarrasses me to know that my own father worried that my face was so plain it could scare away suitors. A father should think his own daughter beautiful, shouldn't he?" she asked.

"Yes," said Ivana quickly.

It soothed Talia's anger. The blood red of her cheeks cooled to a faint blush hardly noticeable against her darker skin.

As for me, I thought that a father who could see his daughter clearly, faults and virtues, was very wise indeed. And it frightened me a bit to think that I had set myself against this same father, and between him and the two girls he now thought of as daughters. Well, I would just have to work more swiftly than he expected.

"But Duke Fensky thought it cruel for me to have no

hint of the man I was to marry. Father was adamant that we not meet until the engagement was well known, so the duke decided he would send me letters instead, to acquaint himself to me."

"So," I said. "Your father seemed to care as much about your opinion on the matter as on a mare's choice of a stud. Did you never once tell him about your love for Blenin?"

Talia raised her hand to strike me. It was only at the last moment that she let her hand fall down. "I did not meet Blenin until after the engagement with Duke Fensky was settled," she said.

And likely she was content enough with it at first. It was only later that she began to have questions. Well, she was right to.

"But my father loves me," said Talia in a low voice. "He would not do anything to hurt me."

"Of course not," said Ivana. She glowered at me.

Now I had united them against me. It was not at all what I wanted.

"It is only that he wants the best for me," Talia went on. "And with his reputation, there is no doubt about Duke Fensky's honor, his wisdom, or his wealth."

Unlike Blenin, I presumed.

"I do wonder if I should feel sorry for him, though," said Talia after a moment, looking more reflective than I had ever seen her. She seemed to act, speak, and even come to conclusions without much thought.

"Why?" asked Ivana.

"Because he doesn't have any idea whom he'll be marrying," said Talia. She put her hands to her face, as if expecting to find it unchanged.

It made me feel a moment's pity for her. She had always been ugly, as I had been. And the promise of beauty—no matter who offered it or at what price—had been too much for her. If my sister had offered me her body whole, would I have rejected it to be my old self?

"You have written no letters in return?" asked Ivana.

"No," said Talia.

Ivana sighed relief. I think Talia did not understand it. "If you had written to him, then it would be you he would expect to marry."

I did not say that Minitz had already described his daughter to the duke and that Ivana would never fit that description. The truth was, I did not think it mattered. It sounded as though Duke Fensky was a paragon of every virtue, but I still did not believe it. Such a man would look for a matching paragon, and neither Ivana nor Talia had ever been that.

Ivana held out the first of the duke's letters. She ignored me entirely and spoke only to Talia. "What does it say?"

Talia was puzzled for an instant.

I suppose I was in a mood to make everyone angry that night. "She cannot read," I said, to make things clear.

"Oh," said Talia.

Ivana pressed her lips further together. She was not likely to have learned to express her anger more openly at home with her father. Not like Talia.

At least Talia knew enough not to make a fuss over this. Instead, she simply read aloud:

My dear Talia,

I write this letter in the hope that we might become somewhat acquainted. I wonder what it is you would wish to know of me. My past?

No. That is nothing. My future? How can I know that until you are with me? So it must be the present. I will tell you what I do each day, what I enjoy, what I do not. And perhaps sometime you will do the same for me.

There followed an account of the man's daily life. He seemed to spend most of his time thinking of the poor around him, and it was clear that he did not treat his servants as beneath him. Rather, they were more family, but perhaps that was because they were all he had. He said nothing of his mother or father, and I presumed this was because they were long dead. If he had any siblings, he did not mention them.

I thought over the man's strange view of the world. The queen had always taught me that those with power used it to control those without. It was the way of the world. But this man either refused to believe it or was too stupid to see the possibilities. I could not see that he was stupid in any other way, however. Certainly his writing was filled with charm and humor, though he was rather closed with his own feelings about the events he discussed. I had thought to find the man's defect in his writing, but instead I could only guess at it. Did he truly see no difference between himself and Talia? It seemed so.

Talia finished with the first letter and folded it back up and put it with the others. She seemed to be thinking, then she turned to Ivana. "You are no merchant's daughter," she said, not in accusation, but in revelation. "A merchant's daughter would have been taught to read."

Ivana gave up with a sigh. "No, I am not." And if that were not enough, she added: "Nor is my father dead by bandits. I come from a village far from where you came upon me. I fled my father and the marriage he had planned for me to an old farmer, Vanye."

"A marriage he had planned for you?" echoed Talia.

Ivana nodded, and Talia's shoulders began to shake. I thought at first she was weeping, then I heard the sound of hysterical laughter.

"Ha—ha—" wheezed Talia. "It is so funny, so funny."

"I do not understand." Ivana looked to me, as if I could help her with this. But a magic mirror cannot cure madness, only disguise it.

"You do not see it?" Talia wiped at the tears on her face and breathed deeply. "How there seems to be no other choice for us than marriage? You ran from your father because he tried to force you to marriage. And with your magic mirror, you made yourself into me. I let you, because I did not wish to be forced to marriage either. Yet we will both still be married. Do you see the joke now?" Talia tried to hold her hand to her mouth, but the laughter was too strong to hold back.

Ivana went pale. "Will the duke beat me, then?" she asked, as if she could understand no other reason for Talia to dislike the idea of marriage so much.

Talia's laughter died away and her voice was all seriousness. "No. I do not think the duke would hurt a fly. You have only to read him go on about his gardens, and the way he refuses to kill the wasps in his yard. He says it is because they will eat other vermin, but I think it is because he does not like to kill anything."

Ivana took a moment to take that in. Her color seemed better. "And is he old?" she asked next.

"Near thirty, or so he tells me." Talia waved at the letters. "I have no reason to disbelieve him."

"Vanye claimed to be sixty-seven," said Ivana, matter-of-factly. "But no one believed he could be so young. He had no teeth, you see, and he wrapped his few hairs around his head like a woman's bun."

"Oh," said Talia. She looked displaced, as though Ivana's words had painted a new world more different than even my magic could have conjured. But the truth was, Ivana thought a man who did not beat her and was in his thirties was the perfect husband. He would have to have been a monster in some other way for Ivana to even think twice.

After a moment, Ivana shuffled through the letters, then handed the whole stack back to Talia. "I still cannot read them," she said. "You may as well have them back."

Talia took them and rose to leave. Then she stopped and turned back to the bed. She sat on a corner and beckoned. "Come sit with me and I will read them to you."

"You will?" Ivana smiled wide enough to break her face.

"If you trust me to read them true," said Talia.

Apparently, Ivana did. And so Talia read. On and on.

The letters were much the same as the first. Ivana was right that the man had an unnatural need to keep even the smallest things alive. He spoke of the worms in the earth and the butterflies, insects, spiders all with nearly the same warmth and intensity that he used for his servants.

"So, what do you think of him?" Talia asked when she had come to the yawning end.

I thought the man odd, but Ivana was fairly glowing with excitement. "He sounds wonderful!"

"Does he?"

I wondered at Talia's pause if she would decide to change her mind. The duke, for all his whims, seemed better and better.

But Talia shrugged. "I welcome you to him, then."

Ivana stood. "Thank you for reading the letters to me."

"If you would like," Talia said slowly, the first sign of hesitancy I had ever seen in her. "I could teach you—how to read."

"Me?" asked Ivana. She shook her head. "No. Impossible. I am even too stupid to learn how to cook a good meal."

It sounded like something her father had said to her, and it reminded me that I had not yet mentioned the cook's magic to her. Well, there would be time enough for that tomorrow. And who knew—if Talia was interested in helping Ivana with reading, perhaps she could be convinced to help her with magic as well.

"It is really quite simple," said Talia. "If you can learn to use a magic mirror, I think the alphabet should not challenge you unduly."

A glimmer shone in Ivana's eyes. "You think I could, then?"

"Of course," said Talia. She got out one of the letters again. "Here. This is an *F*." She pointed to Fensky's signature. "Look over the rest of the letter. Do you see any other marks like it?

Ivana's brow was furrowed. She looked up and down the page, squinting. She looked again at the *F*, tracing her finger over it.

Talia seemed to be holding her breath, for there was no sound at all from her.

Finally, Ivana's finger hit the paper with a sound like thunder. "There," she said. "There it is."

Talia bent over the paper and nodded. "If you can see that, you can learn to read," she said. "All it will take is time, and a good teacher." She smiled at the compliment to herself.

"What's next?" asked Ivana. "Tell me more."

Talia yawned, not entirely in pretense. "Tomorrow," she said. "We'll rest tonight and work again tomorrow. But we must be careful. My father thinks you—I—already know how to read. We'll have to meet in secret. We'll tell him we're discussing a trousseau." Her eyes turned dreamy. "A trousseau, yes." She wandered out of the room, and Ivana put out the light.

Chapter Ten

IN THE MORNING, Ivana woke at dawn. She must have been used to it from her days on the farm. She lay in bed, quietly watching the sunrise.

"Good morning," I said, taking advantage of the moment.

She stretched and pattered toward me. "Mirror." She tucked me under an arm, then brought me back to bed with her. "Do you like it here as much as I do?" she asked.

"Minitz is generous," I said.

"And Talia," said Ivana.

Well, since I wanted Talia to work with Ivana, I could not gainsay this. "Do you ever wish for your old face back?" I asked instead.

Ivana held my glass closer to her face now, surveying her new features. I had thought them plain originally, and so they were. But they had grown on me. The pale lips were pleasantly plump. The eyes seemed to change in light, sometimes green, sometimes brown. The sharp nose was something to grow into, perhaps. Ivana did not have quite the temperament for it yet.

"If I had not been so pretty," said Ivana, "Old Vanye would not have wanted me to wife."

"Well, there are certainly disadvantages to being pretty, but all in all, I would think you would prefer it to being plain."

Ivana shook her head slowly. "If I changed my face back, I would not be a merchant's daughter anymore. I would not be marrying a duke. Think of it! I'll never be hungry again. I'll have fine clothes to wear every day of my life. I'll be clean!"

I wasn't sure which of the three Ivana would like the best in the new position she was expecting. "Yes, I can see why you would not want to give up any of those things. But now that you seem safe here, I wonder if you might like a small change."

Her eyes turned to a light green with faint specks of brown. They were wide and afraid.

"Not like before," I added hastily. "Not at all the same. I mean only a few differences, here and there. Make your cheeks glow, heighten the blue in your eyes, define the chin."

Ivana put a hand palm down under her chin, pulled

back some skin and looked at herself again.

"It would be the same face," I said. "Only better."

"Mmmm," she said.

"Many of the noble ladies do the same thing, but without magic," I went on. I remembered this from the days of the queen. She had often seen women with false color on their faces. Whenever they came into her presence, she was sure to use her magic to strip them down to their true faces. It was an interesting facet of the queen that she would use magic to change herself but thought other artifice a lie.

"They do?"

"And why not?" I asked, thinking of the duke. "Their husbands will want them to look their best on every occasion."

Ivana took another moment, but by then I knew I had her. I was not surprised when she nodded and held herself still once more. "All right," she said. "You may do it."

I let the silence fill her with desire. Then I told her, "Ah. There's the problem. You see, I used the last of my magic on your hands. I haven't any more."

"Oh." Ivana let me drop to the bed.

"But if you got more magic for me . . ."

She pulled me back to her face. "How?" she asked, her eyes alight with eagerness.

I suppose she thought that I had been born with the

magic I had. She had no idea how to gather more, and it was partly my fault for keeping her ignorant of it. "The cook," I said.

"She has magic?"

"Some," I said. The truth was, I was afraid of the great magic I had sensed here. I did not know if I could face it. It seemed to me a good test, to see what the cook had, and if I could take it without difficulty. Either way, it would help me for the battle to come.

"Will she give the magic to me, then? If I ask her?" The rising sun had caught her face now, painting it a luminous peach it would have at no other time of day. Like this, Ivana was almost beautiful still.

"I did not plan on you asking her," I said.

There was a pause.

"You mean—steal it from her?" She turned away from the light, and her face was plain as tin. She needed me still.

"With Talia's help," I said. "I'm sure she knows the cook's habits and other useful details."

"Oh—would she help me, do you think?"

"Did you not say she was a friend? Almost a sister now?"

Ivana wavered.

"If you have difficulty convincing her, you have only to remind her that if the duke decides he would rather have a beautiful girl instead of a plain one, her father could easily change his plans."

"Oh, no," said Ivana immediately. "I couldn't tell her that. It would make her afraid."

Precisely. I sighed. "Tell her what you think you must, then, to get her assistance."

It did not take much. After a little while a maid came in to help Ivana dress for breakfast. She went without me. But after breakfast, Ivana did what I had bid her and brought Talia back. I let them spend an hour or so with reading.

Talia taught Ivana the first five letters of the alphabet, as well as the sounds they made. I recalled the days when Zerba had insisted that I learn to read. In the middle of the hottest summer, the second year of my apprenticeship with her, she had called me inside every afternoon and made me sit with her. I had twisted and fidgeted until she was forced to put spells of stillness on me to keep me from driving her mad.

"Why isn't my sister learning to read as well?" I asked.

"Because she sees no reason for it," Zerba said.

"That's because there is no reason for it!" I fought the spell for long enough to stand up and stomp my foot, but I couldn't last against it and was soon sitting docilely on Zerba's floor once more.

"There is a good reason for it," Zerba said calmly.

"Oh? What?"

Zerba took a dusty book off her shelf and handed it to me.

I stared at the scrawling ink. So many letters—I could hardly imagine reading them all.

"This is a book of spells from the best wizard of the last century. He died without leaving a single one of his apprentices alive."

"He should have protected them better," I said. That was one of the responsibilities of a full-grown witch or wizard to an apprentice.

"Perhaps," Zerba agreed, but she was not sidetracked. "But he left this book instead, and I think it better than any number of apprentices." She stared at me.

I was quick to defend myself. "But why? A book cannot help fetch water or gather herbs or go buy food from the villagers," I said.

"No, that is true," said Zerba. She put the book down on her table heavily. It made a deep sound, like bread that did not rise properly—as was often the case in Zerba's hut. She had magic for many things, but she did not use it on her bread. And neither she nor I nor my sister had ever learned how to bake.

"But a book does not forget how best to use the magic from a ferret, or a rat. A book does not try to improve a magic object whose power has been tried and true. And a book has no reason to lie to keep its secrets safe."

Zerba gave me a moment of silence to think this over. I did, and realized she was right. I reached for the book and looked at the first word. "Trans—" I began, but gave up at the length of it. It seemed impossibly long.

"Transformation," Zerba finished for me.

I shook my head in despair.

Zerba patted my head. "You will learn it soon enough," she said. "Give yourself time and the words will be as easy to you as they are to me—as easy as following after your sister in the middle of the day." She looked at the door, and I saw my sister there.

"Must she stay here?" my sister asked.

"One day you may be glad she knows how to read," said Zerba.

My sister snorted. "I doubt it."

"You think you will never need help with your magic."

"If I do, then I am dead," said my sister. "And I don't plan to be dead."

Zerba let me go then, but I could feel her eyes on both of us, watching as we went into the woods to gather some new magic that my sister had found, in the form of a deer with a broken leg wandering too far from the stream to reach a drink. A few hours and she would have been dead. But we got to her first, and my sister took the magic into herself, forming it into beauty. She turned her eyes to a piercing green, as deep as life itself. And she gave me enough to slim the bulk of my torso, though she did not shorten it or make it fragile as was hers.

"You see? I do not need books with my magic," said my sister.

At the time, I thought she was correct, for I could not imagine when my sister would ever need the help of some other practitioner of magic. She had to be independent in all things. As for me, I went back the next afternoon and learned more letters from Zerba, day after day, month after month, until I could read the book of spells that Zerba had on her desk as well as Zerba herself. I found that I never had enough magic to put the knowledge to use, however. And when Zerba died, the book mysteriously disappeared by the time I thought to ask my sister about it.

Ah, what did it matter now? I might not have forgotten how to read, but I had no hands to turn pages and no magic to make spells.

"Very good," said Talia as Ivana read the first word of one of the duke's letter.

Ivana smiled, shyly pleased with herself. "Thank you," she said.

"It is nothing," said Talia.

"It is not nothing," Ivana insisted. "You have been very good to me."

"Well, perhaps you deserve it. It sounds as though life with your father did not give you many pleasures."

"I had no idea . . ." Ivana's voice trailed off. She stared at the room again, the ease she had found turning to awe. "You could have left me on the road," she said. "But you didn't. And I repay you by taking your face—your life—your father—your home."

No—now was not the time for a drippy scene of remorse. Let it come later, if it must, but not now that I needed action.

"My betrothed," added Talia quietly. "Don't forget that you took him too. And gave me the chance at true love that I have always dreamed of."

But Ivana would not let it go at that. "I did not mean to give you that," she said.

Talia, at least, was not the stickler for noble intentions that Ivana was. "You did it nonetheless. And besides, my father loves you now. It would hurt him if I did anything against you."

"You think so?" asked Ivana, the awe overpowering her again, to tears. "You think it is not just his love for you?"

"He loved me—loves me still, I hope—" Talia looked down at herself. "But we were always arguing. You do not know how often. We argued about what the cook would make for breakfast, some days, and about what the weather would be like when we stepped outside."

"And who won?" asked Ivana. "When you argued?"

Talia looked pleased with herself. "Well, I did." She frowned and looked out the window at the rich colors of the fields beyond. "Except about marriage. Father was always telling me he thought arrangements best, and no matter how I tried to convince him I could choose for myself, he did not listen. And then, there was Duke Fensky."

Turning back to Ivana in the sallow room, she said, "You saved us both from those awful battles. I didn't know how to stop myself, but now that I am another person, it is easy enough. I think my father and I love each other better now, in many ways. And I thank you for that, Ivana."

Perfect! Now was the moment to make a request. Such a small thing—she could hardly refuse.

But Ivana had to first fold up the letters carefully, tie them with string, and return them to Talia. I made a small noise like the clearing of a throat. Ivana heard it, stilled, and steadied her shoulders. "I have a favor to ask," she said.

"Yes? What is it?"

"My mirror—it needs magic." She swallowed, and I thought she would keep the rest to herself. But no, the compulsion to truthfulness had bit her well and truly now. "I want it to make me a little more handsome.

Not for my sake—I don't care. But for the duke."

"I doubt he would care if you looked like a horse," said Talia.

Ivana flinched.

So Talia softened her tone. "But if you wish it, I suppose it would be hypocritical of me to say I don't understand why." Talia looked back at her old face.

I took the opportunity to explain my plan. "Your father would think it nothing more than you growing older, growing up. We would do them gradually."

Yes. This had come at the spur of the moment, but it was just right. No matter how much magic I got from the cook, I would only do one change in Ivana. Then I would tell her I needed more to do the rest. And more again. She would be caught by then, in her hope to attract Duke Fensky, then to hold him to her. She would not dare to stop.

"And where will we get this magic?" Talia turned to me instead of Ivana. Her eyes were far sharper than they had been when Ivana wore them.

"The cook," I said.

"Ah." Talia breathed out heavily. "The cook. Well, I can't say I would be sorry to see her magic gone."

"That means you will help us?"

Talia turned away from me and looked directly at Ivana. "I will help you," she said, making her feelings for me quite clear. "Because you asked me to. And because I wish you all the luck in the world with Duke Fensky."

Of course she did. Above all, Talia would want to make sure that Duke Fensky was happy with Ivana. If he was not, there might be questions. And then the truth would be out about Talia as well.

But Ivana did not think of this. She was enthusiastic in her thanks a second time that morning. I paid no attention to them, though I did listen when Talia said that before dinner would be the best time to investigate the cook's bedroom.

"She'll be busy burning the food," said Talia. "While she drinks her tea and reads the leaves for her future."

"It is her apron I need," I said. Which would be around her waist if she were cooking—or pretending to do so.

"In that case," said Talia, "after dinner. She will leave the dishes for the morning, as she always does." Her nose wrinkled in distaste. It would have looked better on her old face, with the more defined nose. With Ivana's nose, the gesture seemed somehow muted, unexpressive.

"After dinner, then," said Ivana. And so it was.

Chapter Eleven

THAT EVENING dinner was in the dining hall. I sat in Ivana's lap throughout the meal, seeing half the scene and guessing at the rest.

There was a single servant to bring us food, a young girl who kept her face hidden under a bonnet as if she knew that I was curious to see her. A stream of magic ran from the food back to the kitchen, almost visible to me as a streak of green and blue. Steam rose from each dish like billows of clouds—that was magic, as well. Without it, the meal would have been stone cold. As it was, Ivana ate too hastily and burnt her tongue.

She waved a hand over her mouth to cool it off, and I thought again how little like a merchant's daughter she still acted. She had the gown of a merchant's daughter, a fine pale green with embroidered flowers running up the sides in elongating lines. Her face had been powdered and pinched and her hair towered above her head in a dangling spire of braids. The plain face I had seen at first seemed lost in Ivana's happiness. She was at the very least handsome now.

Talia's face, given the same care, was perfection itself. But her gown, unfortunately, did nothing to add to it. She was dressed in one of her old dresses, which the maid had passed down to her. The color was a pale pink that would have looked well on Ivana's new pale skin, but seemed washed out on a darker complexion. Though Talia was not as dark as she had been at first. Some of Ivana's color had been from being out in the sun so long, and now that she was indoors, it had faded.

As I looked at them from my vantage point, I thought it interesting that the two seemed to be growing alike, and in more than looks. Ivana had more spirit than she'd had, though not as much as Talia. And Talia seemed to know that there were moments to be quiet. Not now, but other moments.

"I wonder how Cook does it," said Talia with a touch of sarcasm. "All the food so hot. It is a miracle."

"She is a miracle," said Minitz. "But she is ours." He smiled broadly, then bent his head to the plate to eat again. He did not try to keep from making noises while he ate, and even I had several rather clear images of what the food in his mouth looked like half-masticated. The wealth of a nobleman he might have, but Minitz was of a different class entirely. He seemed to find no greater delight than in his food.

No wonder, I thought, that he had not been impressed by the simple cooking of the woman at the inn. She had used no magic on her food, only the tricks of her trade. And in comparison to what he ate at home, anything unmagicked would taste incomplete.

"And how have you spent your day?" asked Minitz when his appetite was slaked. He leaned back in his chair and placed his hands over his stomach, as I had seen him do so many times before, when satisfied with himself.

"Oh, talking together. Planning our trousseaus," said Talia, as planned. "And what of you, Father? I noticed you were gone early this morning."

"Ah, well. I had our goods to take to market," said Minitz.

"Did you do well?" asked Talia.

Minitz's eyes twinkled. "As always." He then went through a long report of every item in the wagon, down to the six and a half dozen penny nails. He explained how much he had spent for all in the south, and how much he had sold them for in the north. "Now," he said, turning to Ivana, "you tell me what my profit was."

I wondered if it was a test to trap Ivana. What would happen when she failed it—for I knew she would.

Ivana's mouth quivered. She had never learned her letters, much less her numbers.

Talia cut in bravely. "Do you mean including the cost of the journey itself?" she asked.

"No," said Minitz. "I had not yet thought of that." His brows furrowed as he calculated. His thick fingers moved up and down and he whispered to himself.

While he was thus distracted, Talia leaned over and whispered to Ivana: "Five hundred sixteen gold pieces."

Ivana nodded, her eyes wild with desperation.

Minitz nodded and looked up. "The journey was of little importance—only sixteen pieces of gold. So—tell me my profit. You have always been better at math than I." He turned to Talia, bragging. "Some of my sellers think to steal from me by tricking my daughter, when I send her in my stead. They are always sadly surprised at her exactness. Well—?" He turned back to Ivana.

Her lips were nearly purple, they were so bloodless with fear. "Five—five—" she stuttered. "Five hundred . . ." She would have said the sixteen as well, but Minitz slammed his fist on the table first. The clatter of dishes was enough to cover Ivana's bleat of terror.

"Correct!" he said with pride. "Five hundred gold pieces. Not a bad profit for six weeks' work. A portion of that will make a handsome addition to your dowry," he added.

Ivana had no breath left from her scare to speak, but Talia was more used to the merchant's ways. "But I thought that the duke was already wealthy," she said casually. "I thought he had told you there was no need for a dowry."

Minitz looked from Talia to Ivana and back again. I could not see his expression, but something in it made Ivana stiffen, if only for a moment. "I see you did talk a good deal today." His voice sounded affable enough.

"Yes, we did, Father," said Ivana.

The servant cleared the first course of dishes and brought freshly roasted boar. The merchant said nothing, and my attention turned away from his game of entrapment to the cook and her magic. I was certain from the smell of the magic around the silver platter that the meat was not boar. What was it? Horse? Dog? I did not think the cook above either of those. Or perhaps it was not any kind of meat at all, but swollen wheat formed into the shape of boar.

Minitz ate heartily again, Talia less so. Ivana again followed the merchant's lead. After a long belch, Minitz nodded to the servant, and she took his bloody plate away and brought him a flagon of ale. "Ah." He patted his stomach, then tapped his fingers on the table. "The dowry," he said again. "It is true that the duke has said there is no need for a dowry. I wondered if you would wish one anyway. So that you would have money for your own use, once you are married."

Ivana's head went down. She looked at me, and I longed to shout at her to grab her chance while she had it. But she already felt such guilt over taking Talia's place—she could not accept any more. "I have no need for a dowry," she said. "Perhaps she should have it instead."

"Ivana?" Minitz looked at Talia. "Will there be a need to pay a dowry for your marriage? I had thought your father would have settled that already."

Talia cleared her throat noisily and her eyes swirled dark blue in panic. "No, no," she said, keeping her voice from shaking. "They were negotiating still."

"Negotiating still? Well then, to my mind, you have no obligation to go through with it, if you do not wish it."

"I will do as my father wished," said Talia stiffly.

"Ah, then. For a daughter who is so committed to her father's memory, I could hardly do less than offer a dowry for her sake." He turned to Ivana, and I began to suspect this was another part of the game. He intended to make them both as uncomfortable as possible, in repayment for the discomfort that caused him. "What do you say to half our profit from this trip, Daughter?"

Ivana said nothing. I think she was still trying to understand what half of five hundred gold pieces would be.

"It is more than generous," said Talia, who did

understand. Then she added, tearily, "Father."

I could see his massive shoulders relax. The game was given up for the moment. Minitz put his hand across the table and held hers. "Do not cry. Please, do not cry."

Ah, well. Talia seemed to recover herself quickly. The merchant patted her hand and she sniffed once—twice. Then smiled again at her father. "Thank you," she said softly.

The merchant stood suddenly. "I must go write in my books." He nodded to Ivana. "Once I had a mind like my daughter's, and I would not forget my numbers. But no more." He took one last gulp of ale then slammed down the mug and moved to the door.

I felt my hope rise again in his absence. Hopefully, the confrontation I expected would not be tonight. Perhaps not ever.

The servant girl began to clear the table, and Talia stood. She lifted her own plate and moved toward the kitchen.

"Miss—" said the girl, putting a hand out to stop Talia.

"Oh, please, Katye. Let us help." Talia had as winning a manner with her servants as she did with her father.

It was not what the queen would have done to get me into the kitchen with the cook. Then again, the queen would never have needed to steal from a cook.

"But—" Katye said. It was obvious she'd never had to deal with such an offer before.

Before the girl could say more, Talia motioned to Ivana to follow her. The two of them took their own plates to the kitchen, then came back for more. In no time, the table was cleared. Ivana brought me to the kitchen with her.

"Would you like us to help you wash?" asked Talia as Katye bent over for a bucket to fill the basin with water.

Katye jumped up, startled. Her mouth hung open like a door broken on its hinge.

"I could fetch the water," Talia suggested.

"Oh, no, Miss," said Katye, clearly dismayed. "That's not your place." And she ran outside, bucket thumping against her thighs with every step.

"Now, hurry!" said Talia as soon as Katye was gone. "The apron must be here somewhere." She began by looking in all the cabinets. Ivana crouched down on hands and knees and searched in cracks and crevices. She was the one who found it, of course. She had a better idea of the cook's mind, I think.

"Here it is." Ivana pulled out the carefully folded blue apron from underneath a barrel of potatoes.

"Good." Talia had barely the chance to tuck the apron under her skirts before the servant girl returned with her bucket of water for washing. A drop splashed on the floor just as Talia moved toward the door. She slipped and caught herself only by grabbing onto poor Katye's arm. The bucket of water spilled all over the floor.

Talia hung her head. "I'm sorry, so sorry."

Katye was drenched but could hardly express anger in her position.

"We will get out of your way. I can see we were really of no use at all. You have by far more experience with your job. I should never have thought to interfere in it." Talia's babbling apology continued even after the door to the kitchen was closed behind us and we had begun up the stairs.

"My room," said Talia when Ivana stopped in front of her own door.

So we went to Talia's room. It was smaller than Ivana's, and the furniture was not as finely made. The view from the window was of the end of the courtyard, and the stables. Talia yanked the apron from under her skirt and threw it on the bed.

"Now, for the mirror." She put her hands out.

Ivana filled them with me.

"Do it, Mirror," said Talia, impatiently. "Take the magic from her. You do not know how I hate her."

There was a story there, and probably one of many that Ivana would need to hear. But for now, my magic. I felt toward the apron.

"Well?" asked Talia, impatient.

"A moment," I said. I wanted to make sure that there was no trap in this magic. I thought it highly unlikely, but it seemed in my best interest to be sure. And of no particular disadvantage to take the time to do so.

But there was nothing. No dark magic around the edges of the apron, no other magic in it at all. So I let myself suck it in. It was a strange feeling, not at all like the life stolen from the fish. Was this smaller or weakened in some way? Well, at least I felt less hungry than before, as though I had taken a drink of water on an empty stomach. I knew it would not last long, but it was better than nothing at all.

"Do you have it?" asked Talia.

"I have it," I said.

Talia pushed Ivana forward, as if afraid that I must use the magic immediately or send it back.

Ivana closed her eyes and held me close to her chest. I could see her pulse throb in her throat. I could feel her heart beating under her ribs. And I changed her again.

It was not my most extravagant use of magic. But not every jewel must be a diamond to be beautiful. There are sapphires and rubies and emeralds, and some people even prefer simple colored stones on their necks like jade or onyx.

With Talia's face, Ivana had been a simple river stone. But now I made her eyes rounder, her cheeks more prominent. I gave a touch of color to her pale lips. But no more than that. It was a good start, and I had no reason to use all my magic. Ivana was a bit of opal now, plain white on the surface, but with flashes of iridescence underneath.

"Ah," said Ivana as she blinked her eyes open and saw the subtly changed face she now wore.

"Let me see," demanded Talia. She pushed me away and took Ivana's chin in her hand. She twisted her face this way and that. "Not bad," she said. "Not beautiful, but not quite plain anymore, either."

Was there a touch of envy in the voice? I had best be careful not to make Ivana too beautiful in her Talia-face. It would tempt Talia to change back, and that would be disaster for us all.

"Is there no more magic?" Talia asked, looking down at me at last.

"No more," I lied.

"Well, no matter. I say it was a good trade regardless. Even if her magic had been thrown to the birds to peck at like bad bread, it would have been worth the effort to ruin that cook."

"Why?" I asked. It was all the encouragement Talia needed to pour out her story.

"She was not content to be cook. She thought she could be mistress of the house, as well," she spat out. "And all this, not two years after my mother died. I was but six years old at the time. My father was still weeping every night. But the cook would come up to his bedroom with a cup of hot tea. I caught her there once, sitting on the edge of his bed, leaning over him so that he could see all she had to offer—" Her fists clenched at this.

"I ran at her and made her spill the tea on herself. She shrieked in pain, and there were burns all over her skin, anywhere she had not been fully clothed. My father was furious with me. I tried my best to make him understand what I had done, but he would have none of it. He made me stay in my room for three days. He would not even let me come out for meals. And then, when my punishment was over, he made me stand in front of her and apologize. Me—" she choked. "Apologize to her!"

"How awful," said Ivana.

It might have been wiser for me to appease her as Ivana did. But I could not bear it. "Did you ever think it might be good for your father to find another woman to share his life with? There are some men who need a woman, after all—"

Talia's response was quick and fierce. "The only woman my father needed was my mother. And once she died, I was all he had left of her."

"I see," I murmured.

"Did she ever do anything like that again?" asked Ivana.

"Not that I knew of," said Talia. "But I am sure she is

only waiting until I am out of the house until she tries again."

And of course Talia, even if she left her father's house, thought she should rule it still. He had spoiled her far too long, and this was the result he deserved.

"A cook with my father," Talia said fiercely, though under her breath. "The shame of it!"

As if another woman would have been more acceptable to her.

"Well, I will take it back down to the kitchen, to make sure she does not have the chance to accuse me." Talia picked up the apron in her hands. Her teeth were bared, and I wondered if she wanted to use them on the apron.

"You don't think she will guess?" I asked. "That you are the one who has taken her magic?"

Talia smiled at this, though she still looked dangerous. "Of course she will," she said. "But how can she prove it? And if she ever says a word of it to my father, she will be admitting she was using magic all along. He appreciates a good cook very much, but I doubt he would like to wonder if his feelings for her were magicked as well."

Ivana took me out at the same time as Talia, but she did not go down the stairs. Instead, she went back to her room, closed the door, and sat very still, looking into her face. It took me a long while to realize what it was Talia had said to upset her.

A cook with her father. Yes, unimaginable to Talia.

But here was Ivana, ready to marry a duke. And who was she?

"I am more than a cook," said Ivana, as if daring anyone to contradict her. Then her bravado faded. "At least, I thought I was."

Yes, and I had thought I was a woman with a sister. Until I became a mirror, and no more.

Chapter Twelve

FOR THE NEXT few weeks, Talia and Ivana played their parts well. When the merchant or the servants were around, they were new sisters. Ivana copied Talia in manner and speech. But when it came to style, Talia found she had much to learn from Ivana.

As a peasant, Ivana had of course never had the resources to look her best, but she had an innate sense of color and texture. Talia depended on that when her father had a seamstress come for several days and measure and sew and show samples of material for both girls. The seamstress offered a pale yellow that tempted Talia, but Ivana urged a blue or green instead. In the end, Talia relied on Ivana's good sense, and both girls had dresses best suited to their current faces.

When they were alone, the two girls spoke to each other by their true names. I thought of telling them how dangerous it was, but I think they knew it and did it anyway. In addition, Talia taught Ivana day by day, bit by bit, to read. Several weeks passed and Ivana was still struggling with simple words, but she had memorized one of the duke's letters so that she could point to every word and say it aloud to herself. Not the same as reading, but it satisfied Ivana at least.

Another ritual that began was Ivana and Talia coming together at bedtime. After dinner and after both had put on nightgowns and sent their servants away, they would sneak to one or the other's bedroom and sit together and talk. Mostly, Talia talked. She told stories of her past, of the day when she fell into a stream and her father rescued her, about the year she refused to eat any meat because she could not bear the thought of having caused the death of an animal. She told all the merchants' favorite jokes, not one of them remotely funny. Jokes about other merchants, jokes about innkeepers, jokes about horses, and little else. Minitz had a limited vision of the world, though not so limited as Ivana, who had no jokes at all to share.

In fact, there came the day when even Talia realized that she was holding a one-sided conversation and insisted that Ivana tell something of her past.

"What do you want to know?" Ivana asked dully.

"Everything," said Talia enthusiastically. "Every detail."

"When I woke up in the morning, I would go to the stream to piss," said Ivana. "And then I would dig for roots to eat. My father made me bring him enough food for his breakfast before I could eat my own. And then he would start the fire from wood I collected the night before."

"Why didn't you refuse and simply eat the roots while you were away?" Talia asked.

Ivana shuddered at this.

"Tell me," Talia said seriously. "I want to know."

Ivana was silent for a while, then looked up into Talia's eyes and realized she meant it. So Ivana told how she had been tied upside down to a tree and left for two days the first time her father caught her eating roots before bringing them home to him to divide.

"And the second time?" asked Talia, not curious anymore, but determined.

"The second time he held me under the water until I passed out. He told me every second that he would not let me up again ever, that the breath of air I had taken before he pressed me under was the last I would ever have."

A silence followed. Then Talia licked her lips. "But he did let you up?" she asked.

Ivana shrugged. "I don't know if he did it or if I drifted away from him after he thought I was dead, and was pushed out of the water by the force of the current."

"He did not tell you, I suppose."

"When I found my way back to our hut, he never said another word about it. My father was not much for words," said Ivana.

"Oh," said Talia. "I see." After that, she always asked if Ivana had something she wanted to say, a story to share. But she did not insist. And Ivana, like her father, seemed not much for words.

At the end of three weeks, Talia told a story about the first time she made her own bargain. She was five years old, and her father had left her in the wagon as he went inside a shop to speak to a man about the glass bottles he had on display.

"Were you afraid to be left alone?" asked Ivana.

"Ha," said Talia. "I was thrilled. Father was always telling me what I could touch and what I couldn't, whom to talk to and whom to be silent near. As soon as he disappeared behind the door, I hopped out of the wagon and went on my way down the row of stalls. I remember there was a wood-carver's stall, with creatures, deer, moose, elk, bears—but in miniature. I stared at them for a long time, not daring to touch them, even if my father wasn't there.

"Then I went on, to the fruit stall. I could smell the oranges and lemons from a distance, but it was a large spiked fruit that I decided I wanted. I put my nose to the skin, then lifted it in my palm. A little boy ran over to me, shouting at me to stop. I gave him a good stare—" Talia shared an example of it with us then. It was piercing, but it would have worked better had she not laughed immediately afterward.

"He snatched the fruit right out of my hands and put it back on the shelf."

"What did you do then?" asked Ivana.

"I stuck my tongue out at him, of course," said Talia. "And then I told him how much I'd give for the fruit. Five pennies was the price of ten good apples. But the spiked fruit was exotic, so I thought five pennies would be a good beginning. The boy's father came and stood behind him, but he didn't say a word. The boy was in charge of this bargain.

"'How do I know you have five pennies?' he asked first.

"I shook my head at him. 'You don't,' I said.

"'Four pennies,' said the boy."

"Four?" asked Ivana. "But that was less than you offered."

Talia nodded. "But I didn't tell him that. 'Five,' I said again, fierce as a lion.

"'Three,' said the boy."

"What did his father say?"

Talia shrugged. "Nothing. He wanted the boy to learn, I suppose. The boy was older than I was, seven or eight at least. In the end, he offered it to me for one penny, and I took it. I opened my pocket and picked the piece out, throwing it to him while I grabbed the spiked fruit. I ran off with it and got back to the wagon before Father had come back.

"I had planned to save some of the fruit for him, but it was a hot day and the fruit smelled so good. When I bit into it, however, my tongue was cut with the spikes, and I threw it on the ground. Hearing me weeping, Father came out to see what was wrong. I told him the story and he congratulated me on being such a bargainer.

"'A born merchant,' he said.

"I told him I hadn't liked the fruit at all, that the boy had cheated me and I wanted my penny back.

"Father wouldn't have it, however. I was so angry with him I wouldn't speak to him for days. But when I think back on it, there is a sweet taste in my mouth."

"From the fruit?" asked Ivana, confused.

Talia shook her head. "From the victory," she said.

"Ah," said Ivana.

I tried to get Talia to talk about her mother, but she had few memories of her, and most of those were stories her father had told her. When Talia was four years old her mother had died in childbirth. The babe, Merchant Minitz's first and only son, had died as well.

"Father says sometimes that he wishes I had had a father and mother both to grow up with." Talia's expression was rueful. "But it is only when I am not acting properly. Well, if acting properly means having no fun, doing what other people tell you, and never thinking for yourself—I have no interest in it. Though I think that my mother would not have been like that if Father loved her so much. She couldn't have been, because he loves me."

But he loved Ivana too, and she was far less strident. I think the merchant was a man who could love any woman, so long as he believed she had a good heart.

"What about your mother?" Talia asked cautiously. "Do you remember her?"

"A little," said Ivana.

I thought that would be the end of it, but Talia let the silence draw out, and finally Ivana filled it.

"I never knew if she ran away from my father or if he killed her. She kissed me good night one evening, and left me with a tiny tin bead in my hand. I didn't realize it was a good-bye gift until the next morning, when I woke up in the cold hut, my father shouting at me to fetch wood for the fire."

She continued after a moment. "I used to think she would come back for me. For years I would tell myself stories about the home she was making for me, far away from him. I imagined how it would be when she came for me. I would rush into her arms and she would throw me into the air and tell me what a dirty little thing I was. But she would kiss me and I would know she loved me still."

"I am sorry she never did," offered Talia.

"Yes, so am I."

"Mothers are overrated," I added to the glum silence.

"Perhaps. But sisters are not," said Talia. And she embraced Ivana and did not let go for quite some time.

I let the conversations go as they would after that, and they became more and more intimate. I told myself it was to my advantage to have the two girls close. It made Ivana's life more secure, and thus mine, as well.

As I became more acquainted with the area around the merchant's estate, I began to distinguish the great well of magic that had so frightened me from two other sources that were also possibilities. I was almost ashamed that I had taken from the cook, but it had been a good exercise. I could take magic, and I could convince Talia and Ivana to help me do it. It was a good precedent to have set as I decided which of the two more manageable sources of magic to pursue. The one west of the house and a bit south was larger, but as I pondered over what story to tell Ivana and Talia about taking the carriage in that direction, they came to me.

"David has invited us to go duck hunting with him," said Ivana one fine afternoon.

Talia waved to the west. "There is a lake a few miles from the house. There is always game there. And Father says he has an itch for duck meat. But we'd have to ride."

After what the cook had been making without magic, I would think he just had an itch for any kind of meat she had no hand in preparing. But the sky was blue and clear, and it was magic I hungered for more than meat. Magic that had to be close to the lake.

"Perhaps I should stay home with the mirror," said Ivana. She had never ridden a horse before.

"Oh, come now. You said you would not mind so much if the mirror came to keep you company. And you do not want David to suspect anything if you stayed at home."

"I could tell him I was ill," said Ivana. Indeed, she looked nearly as green as the gown Talia had chosen to wear for Blenin.

Talia shook her head. "Being ill would never have kept me out of a duck hunt before," she said. "And besides, I never was ill much."

Ah, so I began to see my role. I was to whisper things to Ivana when Talia could not, to make sure she did not make her true identity obvious.

"Well, when do we leave?" I asked, all eagerness.

"David is waiting for us already," said Talia. And when she held me up to the window I could see David holding three horses near the stables.

"She is to ride?" I wondered if any of the horses would be mild enough for Ivana.

"I will make sure that David gives her the mare," said Talia. "You help her complain about it and David might believe it's real."

Ivana did not look at the horses, I noticed. Instead, she began rummaging through her wardrobe, throwing out a shawl here and a ruined pair of stockings there. "I'll wrap you up," she said. "Then you'll keep safe."

"If you wrap me up," I said, "how will I speak to you?"

Ivana stopped, stood out of the wardrobe, and stared at the heap in front of her. "Must I go?" she asked in a small voice.

"Yes," said Talia.

Ivana turned to me.

"Yes," I said. I thought of several ways she could escape. Break an ankle—I could make it real enough, if I cared to. Break out in the spots of the plague—even David would not want to ride with her then. Or make up some other appointment vital to the upcoming wedding. She could even pick a fight with David, if she wished. Talia was moody enough to do that.

But I offered no suggestions.

"You could be smashed," Ivana said in a doomed tone.

"You will take good care of me," I said. She always had before, and she had less reason then than now.

Talia went to the wardrobe and got out a riding outfit

in tan and one in green. "One for you, one for me. Luckily, we are the same size."

Ivana looked carefully at both, then pointed at the tan one. "But I don't even know how to put it on," she complained.

"Well, the maid will help you—" Talia started. Then she stopped and shrugged. "Or I will, if you'd rather."

"Please."

And so Talia and Ivana dressed together. Once they were dressed, Talia looked so much like the queen that I startled at the sight of her turning to me. I half expected to see a face I knew long dead.

But Talia, for once, was not interested in gazing at her new beauty. "Come," she said simply and headed for the door.

Ivana took one last breath of safe air, then grasped me in her hands and hurried after Talia.

Chapter Thirteen

STANDING WITH the horses patiently, David looked quite different from his wife, Silva. Where she was soft-featured, he had a nose like a hawk's and his bones seemed chiseled into place.

"What's that you have there, Miss Talia?" he asked when the two girls approached.

Ivana held it closer to her than ever.

David, who apparently was used to dealing with Miss Talia's whims, only sighed and looked about on the saddle for a place to tuck me. There wasn't one. He eventually tied a rope around Ivana's waist and lashed me into it.

"There, is that all right?"

Ivana nodded.

"Well, then . . ." He waved at the spirited horse with the intricately carved saddle that clearly belonged to the beloved daughter of the house.

Ivana took a step toward the horse, and it shivered at the smell of her. It was an interesting truth that magic could change scents so that humans did not know the difference, but animals were never fooled. This horse knew that his rightful mistress was Talia, no matter what face she wore or whose name she was called. He turned toward her, nickering.

I wished I could do something to force him to respond to Ivana instead of Talia, but if I tried to magic either girl further, it would only increase his confusion. And what could I do to the horse? As a mirror, my magic was limited to changing what appeared in my glass. I could make the horse taller, smaller, redder, or dappled. But that would do nothing but alert David to my power. It would not help Ivana with the horse.

"She is ill, don't you think, David?" said Talia.

David looked at Ivana's face. "Perhaps another horse, Miss Talia?" he asked. "One not so likely to gallop."

Ivana put a hand to her stomach at the word.

"She will argue with you, though," said Talia, giving hints to Ivana. "She has been telling me how much she loves to ride her Wind."

"Miss Talia, I'll do what's best for you, no matter what you say. You know that about me, I hope." David led Wind to Talia, and the two took to each other immediately. David noticed that, of course. No hiding a horse's preferences to a man who worked with them day and night.

But he only said, "I think he likes you, Miss Ivana. Perhaps he smells Miss Talia on you." The flicker in his eyes made me certain that he and his wife had talked over the similarities in Talia's and Ivana's figures and come to the same conclusion—it was no coincidence.

"I know you don't like Sweetwater as well," coaxed David as he drew the smaller of the horses, with a white star on her head, toward Ivana. "But she served you well in your childhood. She will serve you again today."

"Childhood?" murmured Ivana.

"Yes, well," said David. He was expecting a fight.

"Refuse," I whispered in as quiet a voice as I could manage.

Too quiet, unfortunately, for Ivana to hear me. She stood stone still in front of Sweetwater, and I wondered desperately what I could do. Ivana turned so that I brushed against Sweetwater's side, and at the same moment I began to speak a second time.

The touch of raw magic, even such a small amount as mine, was enough to make Sweetwater balk. And that, in turn, forced David to step forward and take control. He put his arms around her neck and whispered gently in the mare's ear. It was so like Talia on the cliffs. I knew now where she had learned to handle horses.

"She's as afraid of you as you are of her," said David. "I think the other horses have been telling stories about how you misuse them."

Ivana's mouth dropped open. "I—" she stuttered.

"Not that you would ever knowingly harm a horse." He winked. "But sometimes your headstrong nature leads you—and your mount—astray, eh?"

Ivana lowered her head, and David took that as assent. Then, before David wondered why Ivana had not vaulted to her seat, Talia distracted his attention.

"Could you help me?" asked Talia. "I've ridden a horse in my time, but none so fine as this one."

"It is a fine horse," said David. "Isn't it?" And he began reciting the animal's pedigree, a long and laborious process.

"Ivana, put your foot in the stirrup," I whispered instructions. "Yes, that strip of leather on the side of the horse. Then hold to the saddle and pull yourself in."

Anyone watching her would have seen the difficulty she was having, but once she was on the horse, Ivana held herself upright, her back straight, as Talia had taught her was important at all times for a girl of good breeding. She was terrified, but perhaps I was the only one who knew that, since I was so close to the thunderous beating of her heart.

David mounted his horse, a bow and arrows slung

over his shoulder. Then we rode around the grounds of the house slowly. Ivana's heartbeat softened next to my glass. I realized in a few minutes that she was no longer holding so tightly to the horn as she had been.

"And now for the real ride," said David, once we were in the open and the path through the fields ahead was clear. He leaned forward, urging his horse onward. Talia's Wind seemed to need no urging. He knew exactly what to do. Ivana's horse was slower than the other two but tried to keep pace.

"Oh," said Ivana after we had passed by the first golden fields of grain. I thought it was a protest, but then she added, "This is wonderful, isn't it?" Her posture changed just slightly, and then it was as if she had become part of the horse herself.

"You must be a born rider," David called out to Talia as the lake came into view.

But it was Ivana who was the born rider. She did not use the reins to pull Sweetwater to a halt, only her knees. She got off the horse, smoothly enough that David didn't look up from his stringing of the bow.

As for me, I could feel the magic as clearly as David could see the ducks flying overhead. He raised his bow once, and there was a streak of brown in the sky as the duck fell. Then Talia ran for it, and I, stupidly, had never thought of the magic I could take from the duck hunting itself.

When Talia raised the bow that David offered with his assistance, I readied myself to do better the second time. These were small magics, but they were easy to gather and I was in no position to be particular.

"Ho, good shot!" whooped David as the creature fell.

I gathered the magic to me, seeing no reason not to. The magic all around me seemed to stir, but by then it was too late for me to keep myself hidden. I had not thought at all about the danger of being stolen from. I had been too intent on becoming a thief myself.

Ivana stood close to David and Talia, but she did not ask to use a bow and David did not think yet to offer it to her. As for me, I could feel the center of the changing magic coming closer, closer. And then, there she was, hidden in the reeds by the lake, crouched down so that any human who looked at her would see nothing more than a blur of green.

Her features were completely forgettable. She was not ugly, nor even plain, as Talia had been. She was simply—a blank human form. She had a nose, a mouth, two eyes. But there was nothing about any of them that was remarkable. They did not even seem to have a color, let alone a shape.

Yet she had magic. Why did she use it like this?

She leaped toward me like an oversize frog. But her magic was so good that no one thought it odd. It was the ducks they were looking at after all.

I did not realize what the marsh witch had planned, but even if I had, I could not have stopped her. For I did not have the power to guard my magic. The queen had not given me that. So when the marsh witch put out her hand, she sifted out of me the little bit of magic I had left from the cook and the duck.

"Who—?" I asked. But she had leaped away from me before the question was finished. She blended into the scenery once more, and I followed her movements a few more yards, from marsh to tree. Then she was gone. I might have imagined it all except that my magic had been taken.

"She's likely simmering back here with anger, aren't you, Miss Talia?" asked David, finally turning back to offer Ivana his bow.

"Oh, but it was kind of her to let you teach me for a little while," said Talia. She raised her bow and shot down three ducks in a row.

Ha, as if she needed a teacher!

Ivana held the bow gingerly, the arrow notched back. "Move forward," I whispered, for I thought if she moved closer to the ducks she would have a better chance of hitting one of them. Or at least come close enough so that David did not think her afraid of something she had spent all her life loving.

Instead, Ivana slipped into the marshy ground and the

arrow flew out from the bow. It had not been aimed, but it hit true. Not a duck, however. It was the marsh witch I had seen before who had gone down. She had lingered too close to us, in the low-lying branch of the tree I had last seen her in. Now she fell from it, a streak of gray that thumped to the ground.

"What in the name of—?" David said. Then he ran, taking care to avoid the marshiest places.

"Did I get one?" Ivana asked, half-dazed.

Talia helped wrench her feet out of the near quicksand, then half dragged her back to the horses. "You got something," she said.

Coming back, David held the crumpled marsh witch in his arms. I could feel that she was dying. Perhaps it was cold of me, but I took back the magic she had taken from me, and more. It was not as much as I had hoped for. Perhaps I had been confused by the animals with their own magic, or perhaps the marsh witch had used some of what I had sensed at first. In any case, I knew I was still far from my goal. At this rate, I would be a mirror for another hundred years.

"Is it a woman?" asked Talia, staring closely at the face.

Ivana put a hand to her mouth and turned away, but not before she truly sickened and vomited up her breakfast.

The marsh witch was well and truly dead by then.

"A witch, I suspect," said David. "I'd heard there was one hereabouts. I never saw her, though."

"I killed her," Ivana was saying blankly. "I killed another human being."

David humphed. "If you ask me, a witch is more animal than human. That's why she was here, I'm sure. To steal life from the animals, until she became almost one of them."

He was right in a way. But there was more to it than what he saw. The marsh witch had had the skill to be a witch in town. That she had chosen another life meant something. She had come to hate humans, perhaps.

And why should she not? A part of me asked this question and had no answer. In my years as a mirror I had not seen much of humanity to be lauded. Of course, Ivana and Talia were not the worst of my acquaintances, and the merchant seemed to have acquired a few of the better specimens in his own household. But considered on the whole, humanity was not worth the trouble. When I had my body back, and the magic to go with it, I was not sure that I would want any more than the little marsh witch had.

But such a sad end. No one mourned her. The humans thought her an animal, but she had never been one of them, either. Even if she had, they would not have the sense to notice her absence.

"I didn't mean to, but I killed her, I killed her," said Ivana over and over again.

David's voice was matter-of-fact. "Well, in some ways it will be a blessing to all." He got a small spade out of his saddle pack and dug a shallow grave, no more than he might have dug had it been a dog Ivana had shot.

He laid the small body in it, looked at her for a moment, and began to cover her with the rich black soil.

"Wait! No words of solace? No prayer?" asked Ivana.

Talia looked just as stricken, and I thought that in this way, the two girls were alike. Both had tender hearts, even when it came to a witch.

"A prayer for her?" David spat. "Begging your pardon, Miss Talia, but any words of prayer would be more like to curse her than help her. Better for her if God does not see her die. He would only punish her."

I did not believe in God. I never had, even from a small child when my mother threatened me with God's wrath. God could be no worse than my father, I thought, and I did not fear even him anymore.

But when David spoke, I felt empty, despite my magic. I had learned to worship power, to take life from death. But now I wondered if there might be something more to life, and to death, than I had thought before. Something warmer than magic, and more lasting.

Talia came closer to Ivana, and the two began to sob

quietly for this witch they had never known.

David shook his head at both of them, but he did not disturb them until he had strung the ducks to his saddle. Then he helped Ivana and Talia to mount. They rode home somberly behind him. Neither of them spoke of the incident the rest of that day, but by evening they seemed to have regained their spirits.

It took me longer to put the incident behind me. Ivana and Talia had each other to talk to, to drown out their thoughts. But when I went silent, they hardly seemed to notice. I had the marsh witch's magic, so perhaps it poisoned me. But the doubts felt like my own, and I never used the magic I had gained. Instead, I felt for weeks as though I had been buried next to the witch in the marsh. Alone, and unmourned.

Finally, the day came when I asked myself if I still wanted to be human or not. There was only one answer I could truthfully give. But the magic I had would not be enough to give me one finger back. I would have to try for the magic I had felt before, from the cliff where the horses had nearly tumbled to their deaths. It seemed my last chance, and I would take it.

Chapter Fourteen

I THOUGHT TO bring up my continuing need for magic with Ivana after breakfast. Perhaps I waited too long. The meal was as lackluster as it had been since the cook's magic had been stolen. She seemed to have no interest in regaining what she had lost. She hardly did more than stir the bottom of a burned pot of porridge before bringing it to the table.

"Even the inn woman made better food than this," muttered the merchant.

"Perhaps we should go on another journey," said Talia.

Minitz shook his head. "We have marriages to arrange. Yours and your sister's."

"Oh? You've told us nothing in so long we were beginning to wonder," said Talia.

"Well, the duke is preparing his home for a visit before the betrothal becomes official."

"And Blenin?" asked Talia.

It occurred to me then that Talia, though she professed a great love for this man, had not spoken of him for days on end. If she was as much in love with him as she claimed to be, she would have pestered her father every day for news. Instead, she had been content to wait. I think her father's disgust with the cook he had once fancied was more interesting to her than her own wedding.

"Blenin," said Minitz, his tone arch, his eyes watchful. "Blenin will in fact be joining us for dinner this very night."

"What?" Talia shouted.

Minitz nodded. "Yes. He will be arriving this evening and will stay the night."

"But—why didn't you tell me?" asked Talia.

"I am telling you," said the merchant. "Now."

"Oh." Talia stood up, then sat back down, and stood up again. "I will have to get ready. What shall I wear?" She turned to the stairs that led to her bedroom. "What shall we eat?" She turned back, toward the kitchen. "What shall I say to him?" She looked at her father.

"I know what I will say to him," said Merchant Minitz.

Talia stopped and put a hand to her throat.

The merchant said, "I will tell him that he had best make my new daughter very happy in her marriage. Or he will answer to me."

Talia smiled gently at this. Then her hands began to flutter, the excitement overtaking her.

Merchant Minitz laughed. "Go on, now. Both of you, go." He pointed to Ivana, and she stood.

There was no chance for me to mention more magic for the rest of that day. Once upstairs, we moved back and forth from Talia's room to Ivana's, searching for the perfect gown, the perfect gloves, the perfect hat, for each of them. This is a sample of how it went:

"What color shall I wear?" asked Talia.

"Green," said Ivana.

"But green might make me look ill."

"Blue, then," said Ivana.

"Is blue too cheerful, though? Perhaps I should wear yellow."

"Yellow?" said Ivana.

"No," said Talia suddenly. "It must be green. I remember him saying that he missed the green of summer. It was dead winter when we saw him last."

"Green." Ivana sighed in relief. "A good choice."

And so Talia wore the green for a few minutes, until she decided she had best try the blue at least. And then the green again. And Ivana's yellow. And back to the blue.

It was a boring business, and if they forgot to bring me with them each time they went to a different room, I did not feel slighted. I was annoyed that this meeting with

Peter Blenin would take place before I got my magic back, but what could I do about it? I focused on the well of magic and tried to discover what I could about it.

There was a certain taste in it, and I realized after a time that it was familiar. I was intrigued. I dug in my memory for all the witches the queen had ever known. Were any of them this powerful? Could any have lived this long? Or was this the apprentice of a witch I had once met?

I had come to no firm conclusion, though I had thought of some good possibilities when evening came and Talia and Ivana were at last fully dressed and coiffed.

In the end, Ivana wore the yellow and Talia the green, which made her look frail. Or perhaps that was only her nerves. Ah well. The queen always said men liked a weak woman, one who was subservient to their demands. Why should I think Blenin was any different?

From the window came the sound of a carriage approaching. Ivana and Talia went to it immediately, staring out with gasps of excitement at the glory of the carriage and the horses. Talia noticed the fine clothing on the servant who opened the door for Blenin, and then there was silence. I presumed it was because Blenin himself was too marvelous for words.

Finally, there was a knocking, distinct, but distant. Downstairs.

"Oh, I shall die of this," said Talia. She ran to the

door, then came back, then ran to the door again. Her face was splotched in red and white.

"You are afraid?" asked Ivana. She seemed to be surprised, as though the emotion were her sole property.

"Of course I'm afraid. I don't know what my father said to bring him here or what he thinks of me. What if he says he has no idea we are betrothed?"

And miss the dowry that the merchant was offering? From what I had heard of Blenin, even through Talia's love-struck eyes, it seemed extremely unlikely.

"But I thought this was what you wanted," said Ivana. "You have given up so much for him. Why are you not happy?"

A pause, while Talia chewed at her lower lip. "What if what I wanted is not what I wanted?" she asked.

Ivana was baffled. Then her wandering eyes came to me. "The mirror," she said. "You could bring the mirror. The mirror could advise you. Couldn't you, Mirror?"

"For a time," I said. "But I am nearly drained of the cook's magic. If I do not have more soon, I will not be able to speak at all." It was a lie, and not the first I had told to Ivana. It was the first that bothered me, however. She turned to me as a friend, and I responded as an opportunist, as though I had no feelings for her at all. And yet, I did or I would not have felt guilty at my greed.

"Oh," said Ivana, as apologetic as when she had

dropped me into the stream. "I didn't realize, Mirror. What will we do?"

"Go to the market in town," said Talia, pointing in the very direction where I had sensed the magic. "There are always witches there, selling a potion or a cure. It won't be difficult. Father will give us some money, and we will get some magic for it."

The witch I was looking for did not seem likely to be in a market in town, but once we were out in a carriage, I could guide the girls to where I needed to go. And it would not hurt to have a little money, at least to distract the powerful witch when we found her.

"We'll talk about it later," said Talia. "After I meet Blenin."

I did not argue, for there was little point in trying to get useful information out of Talia at this point.

After a few more moments of Talia's dithering, the three of us went down to dinner together. The house was at its best that night. Merchant Minitz had made sure that the dining hall was cleaned, that every corner possible was lit with a dozen candles, that the plates and glasses shone with care. Even the wood of the table had been refinished, a shade darker than before, as if to compliment Talia's dark good looks—Ivana's dark good looks, that is.

"Welcome, welcome, daughters," boomed Merchant Minitz as we walked in.

A tall, well-dressed man at Merchant Minitz's side cleared his throat. He had clear blue eyes and the most extravagant cravat about his neck. It made him look the peacock in my mind. If ever I had suspected a bird of stealing magic from a human, I would have looked first to Blenin for my proof.

"You have met Talia already." Merchant Minitz motioned to Ivana. Blenin barely blinked in her direction. "And this, of course, is Ivana."

Blenin turned to her, and I could see his eyes widen as he took in her beauty. But he covered his hesitation with an elaborate flourish of one hand. "Ah, you are even more beautiful than Merchant Minitz told me. I suppose he must have wished to keep you secret, for fear all the men in the kingdom would be chasing after you." He lifted her hand to his mouth and kissed it far longer than was strictly appropriate, even between a man and his betrothed. "What luck that he chose me."

Talia blinked and stared.

I had thought she would be overwhelmed with his smooth charms. After all, she had loved him before he had ever taken a glance at her. Why not now, when she had all his attention?

"You had not met before, then," said Merchant Minitz. "I did not know that when I wrote to you. I thought things had progressed quite far in the betrothal."

"Not far at all," said Blenin. He let go of Talia's hand at last.

I saw her rub at it. Had he held it too tight? I did not doubt that he was very eager to secure a fortune so easily. No wonder he asked no questions.

"Well then, you are very like my daughter Talia, who has never met the man she is meant to marry. I hope that things go as well for you as I expect they will go for her," said Merchant Minitz.

"Indeed," said Blenin. "I believe they have already gone amazingly well."

Yes, indeed. Whatever the merchant wrote to him, it seemed he had expected a dowdy girl he would have to pretend to appreciate, at least until he could find a way to strip her dowry from her without marriage. But perhaps he would marry Talia after all.

I felt sorry for her at the thought. She had her faults. She was loud and impulsive. She spoke without thinking. She manipulated those she loved and those she did not. She was headstrong and arrogant and spoiled.

But she had also taken Ivana in, and me as well. She had done more for us than we ever would have dared to ask. She had a good heart, and I found that I had become fond of that heart. I did not like to think of it being crushed by a loveless marriage to an opportunist like Blenin. An opportunist? Is that not what I was myself?

Then how would it be better for Talia to stay with me than to marry him?

Because I had come to feel something for her, at least.

"Well, let us begin." Merchant Minitz nodded at a servant near the kitchen, and immediately the food began to appear.

Talia realized at the same moment I did that this array could not possibly have come from the cook. Which meant—"He found a new cook!" Talia whispered happily.

After the first course was served, Talia turned to Blenin. "I hope you traveled well," she said.

Blenin's eyes sparkled at her. "I did indeed. But if I did not, the sight of your brilliant face looking down at me would certainly have erased all memory of mere bumps and jolts along the road."

Talia's mouth lifted at the compliment, but she did not blush, and her eyes seemed somehow distant. Blenin's pretty words did not touch her at all. I wondered if perhaps she had heard some rendition of them before, to another woman. It would not be out of the character I saw in Blenin to keep compliments in stock and to use them at will. He would not think to catalog to whom he had said them, and even if he did, he would not know that the girl who was now Ivana had heard them in another guise.

"And what did you think of our valley in the summer?" asked Minitz.

"Ah, I could never see the summer again and not think of Ivana. For the beauties of nature are many, but what rose could compare to the flower of her?" asked Blenin. "She is beyond compare."

If he had said beyond price, I would have begun to choke. The man was as bad as any of the men the queen had ever dealt with, only he had not the station they had. He spoke with a nobleman's affected manner, with a nobleman's phrasing, but he was hardly more than a peasant. Any merchant's daughter would have been above him, and Talia was far more than that.

The second course arrived, and as servants took away his food, Minitz spoke again. "Perhaps you could tell us about your acquaintance with Ivana's father?" he asked.

Blenin's mouth dropped open, revealing several missing teeth. I wondered if they had been knocked out by women who found his flattery annoying, or by men whose wives or daughters had been taken in all too well by it. "Uh—I'm not sure—could you be more specific?" he stuttered.

"Father, please!" said Talia, with a hint of desperation. But looking at her, I suspected it was all for herself and not for Blenin at all.

"Oh, if it is too painful to hear, I am sorry. I should have been more considerate. Forgive me please, my new daughter," said Minitz. I could not tell if there was irony in his pleading gaze at Talia, but his tone was somber enough.

"Thank you, Father," said Talia.

"At another time, I will tell you the sad events of the last months," said Minitz to Blenin. "For now, you need only know that I am in the place of a father to Ivana in the matter of her wedding."

Blenin's fear had dissipated easily enough. "She is a lucky woman in that, at least," he enthused. "As lucky a woman as I am a man." He turned to Merchant Minitz. "And with such a kind and generous man to act as a father-in-law as well, what more could a man wish for?"

A brain, I thought. And a heart.

The third course came: meats and sausages. Blenin ate with careful manners, but he did not stint on amount. The servants brought him three full plates and he cleaned them all. I could imagine him in twenty years, as stout as the merchant was now, but without the courage and strength that gave the merchant's massive figure its form.

"So," said Talia when Blenin was finished at last. "You favor summer best of all the seasons?" she asked.

Blenin nodded and blotted at his lips with a heavy linen napkin. He smiled. "Of course, for it is summer when we met."

"Then what do you think of a summer wedding?" asked Talia. There was a bit of mischief in her eyes, but Blenin did not know her well enough to be wary of that.

For the first time, I began to think that this might be an enjoyable evening, after all.

"A summer wedding? Yes, in a year or two—that would be fine," said Blenin.

"Good," said Talia. "But I see no reason to wait for another summer, do you?"

Blenin spluttered wine all over the tablecloth. "Ah, well—of course—summer is lovely—but—ah—"

For some reason, Merchant Minitz came to Blenin's rescue. "I had thought you would wait for a while, Talia," said the merchant. "To be sure you suit. There is no sense in rushing a marriage, is there?"

Talia's mouth tightened. "No sense in waiting for it, either," she said, challengingly. She turned to Blenin.

He licked his lips. "No, no need to wait." He turned to Merchant Minitz. "Unless others wish us to."

Minitz's shoulders relaxed slowly. "I had thought in the winter," he said quietly. "Near Talia's wedding with Duke Fensky."

Talia was torturing them both, and with the same ploy. What neither of them knew, but which I could see plainly in Talia's stance, was that she had no more intention of marrying Blenin this summer than she had of marrying Duke Fensky.

"It is my wedding," said Talia stubbornly. "I should have it when I want."

Minitz sighed. "If it is truly summer you favor, then I will do whatever is necessary to make it possible."

I wondered then that Talia had not been able to get Minitz to change his mind before I changed her face. But perhaps it was because she had changed her face that he had seen how easily he could lose her altogether.

Merchant Minitz lifted his glass. "To summer weddings," he said, nodding to Talia.

"To summer weddings," said Talia.

"To summer—" was all Blenin could get out.

After a moment, Ivana raised her glass as well. There was a clinking sound as the finest crystal glasses met. Then all drank, though Blenin looked like he had drunk a witch's charm rather than fine wine.

After this, Merchant Minitz introduced more innocuous topics, ranging from the famines in the west to the kingdom in the north, where no king had reigned for years. Blenin must have felt obliged to make some comment, but he only showed his ignorance of anything outside his own region of influence. Talia, on the other hand, had wide-ranging thoughts and the logic to fight for them, if Merchant Minitz demanded.

As the last course of cheese and fruit was taken away, Blenin stood abruptly, allowing his napkin to fall to the floor. He came to Talia's side, knelt beside her, and with a flourishing hand gesture, took her hand to his lips.

"Until the morning," he said smoothly. "Though it seems all too far away."

Well, the man was intelligent enough to know how to flatter, I thought. Perhaps he did not need a brain after all. Only restraint when he used it.

"Thank you," said Talia.

Finally, the man was shown to his room, and Talia turned without a word after him, leaving Ivana and Merchant Minitz—and me—behind.

Chapter Fifteen

TALIA CAME to Ivana's room just after she had changed into her bedclothes.

"I can see why you love him," Ivana offered. "He is so handsome, so charming, so well mannered."

Talia made a face. "He is a snake," she said, proving me right yet again.

Ivana stared. "But the wedding—you said you wanted to marry him before the end of the summer."

"That was only to irritate Blenin," said Talia. Just as I had guessed. "And Father," she added as an afterthought.

You see how well I had come to know her? As if she were my own sister, as well as Ivana's.

"But what is wrong with him?" asked Ivana.

"He is—" Talia waved a hand. "An idiot. No, he is worse than an idiot. An idiot is not so self-interested, so vain." Talia looked to me. "Did you see the way he treated her tonight? As if she were a ghost. Or a servant, beneath his notice. That is the way he would have treated me if not for this face."

"I thought that was why you wanted that face," I said mildly.

Talia stared into the large mirror and pushed and pulled at cheeks, lips, eyebrows. "A face is only a face," she said.

She had changed, I thought. Oh, she was the same in all her best ways, but she seemed to be smoothing the edges off her worst parts. I was proud of her, as if I had had something to do with it all. And I had, in a way. With a new face, she had begun to see herself differently. And so had those around her.

I wondered why it had never worked that way with the queen. At least, I had never noticed it working. Perhaps it was because she had always had the same kind of face, and the changes I made to it had all been incidental. Or perhaps it was because she didn't have the love that Talia had to help her toward a new self. The queen had only had a mirror who had given up loving anyone at all, even herself.

"How will you tell Father, then?" asked Ivana. "If you don't want to marry him, after all."

"You think he'll protest?" Talia shook her head. "Ah, well. I'll think of something. It shouldn't be difficult."

"Do you want to be yourself again?" asked Ivana. Talia did not understand the magnitude of this offer, but I did. To return to her old face, her old self, was what Ivana was most afraid of.

"No," said Talia immediately. "Then I would still be engaged to marry, and Duke Fensky is little better than Blenin."

I didn't think that was a fair assessment of the situation, but I couldn't think Talia would change all at once, could I?

"Is there someone else you want to marry, then?" asked Ivana.

"No one I can think of," said Talia. "Though I'm sure Father could find someone for me, if I asked him." She smiled at this. "But, Ivana, what if I never marry?"

"What else would you do?" Yes, to Ivana there was no question of whether she would marry or if she would have any choice in it. There was only the hope that it would not be as bad as old Vanye.

"Well," said Talia as her face cooled, "Father has been teaching me how to handle his business for years. He has no son to take it over for him. If I married, he would only give it to my husband when he died."

"So?" said Ivana.

Talia spoke fiercely. "It should be mine. And why not? If a man can make a business, why not a woman?"

"Unmarried?" asked Ivana.

"And why not?" asked Talia. "Father used to tell me what a good head I had for numbers. And I have always bargained well. I even know the hands to bribe and the mouths to listen to for news. Why should I give that all up?"

Why indeed? I wondered why my sister had never thought of this. She would not have had to marry those men she so disliked. She would not have had to use them to get her power. She could have found it for herself, but she had never had this flash of insight that Talia had. A woman—not married—on her own.

"If you wish, I suppose you might convince Father to allow it," said Ivana.

Suppose nothing. Talia could convince Merchant Minitz to let her become a sailor if she wished it, or a snow fairy.

"Well, good night," said Talia.

"Good night," said Ivana. When Talia had gone, Ivana stood and put me next to the larger mirror. "Good night, Mirror," she said, as sincerely as she had to Talia.

I watched as she went limp. She still found it easy to sleep. She was used to being too exhausted to do anything else.

Then suddenly, a shriek broke through the night. It was Talia's voice, and I did not think from the sound of it that she was crying out in a dream. Ivana woke up and stared around the room, as if expecting the danger to be near her.

I heard a muffled sound like a voice being stifled, then a low murmur. A man's voice. Then a thumping sound and a crash. Talia getting free, just long enough to shriek a second time.

Ivana ran for the door. "Talia," she cried out, running down the corridor. I heard the man's voice again, as if laughing. Then a smack and a low oath. Then two voices, calling together.

At that point, the whole house awoke. I heard the sound of heavy footsteps down the stairs, and a door slamming.

"Now, get out of this house. And never let me look on you again!" shouted Minitz.

Blenin was not intelligent enough to know when he should go quickly. Instead he seemed to stay to argue about debts and a dowry that was his by right.

"By right!" bellowed Minitz. "By right, your neck should be hanging from my highest oak tree."

Finally, Blenin stopped talking. I heard footsteps again, down the stairs, and then the front door opened and closed and the house was silent.

A few minutes later, Ivana, Talia, and Minitz appeared in the doorway.

"I will kill him," Minitz muttered. "I swear I will kill him if I have the chance."

"Father, he isn't worth it," said Talia. The words were calm, but her voice shook. It was the first time I think I had ever seen her genuinely frightened. She had a livid mark just under her left eye, but there was a kind of power in her trembling. It wasn't with terror. It was with fury.

"To think that he would attack my daughter in my own house."

I noticed at this time of stress Minitz did not mince words about "new" or "adopted" daughter as he had before.

"He said he was 'anticipating our wedding vows,'" Talia spat out. "He said that if I was so eager to be married in summer, I should be eager enough to be bedded tonight."

"He is not a fit husband for a swine," said Minitz. "Not for a bitch or a cow—"

He would have gone on if Talia had not stopped him with a hand on his arm. "I don't want to talk of him," she said.

No one said a word about the father who would have chosen such a husband for his daughter. The truth was, only a daughter, and a very young one, a very stubborn one, would have chosen such a man for herself.

"Please, Father," said Talia. Her breathing was shallow

and rapid. "I want to rest. Only to rest."

"You want to go back in that room alone?" asked Ivana. She too was shaking, but I did not know why.

"No," said Talia, with perfect certainty. She looked around in the room that had once been hers. Since her childhood, if I didn't miss my guess. "Would you mind if I slept here tonight? With you?"

"Of course," said Ivana. "Whatever you wish for, you have only to ask. Do you want me to sleep on the floor? By the door?"

The real Talia would never have offered such a thing. I daresay, from the stunned expression on her face, she would never have thought of it as a possibility. And even Minitz was not too caught up in the events of the night to know this. But he said nothing.

He had to know. He had to. And in the morning, he would tell the truth. He would insist that the girls' faces be returned to those that were rightfully theirs. I would use up all my magic for that, and if I needed more, he would surely give it stingily. What would happen to me then? He would not allow me to remain with them, surely. I was a magic mirror, dangerous, evil, with an agenda of my own. I did not care for his daughters, did I?

"In the bed," said Talia. "You on that side. Me on this one." She gestured right and left.

"Oh," said Ivana, almost disappointed that she could do no more than this.

"Promise me you will not forgive him for this," said Minitz as he moved to the door.

"Ha!" said Talia. "I swear to you, Father, I will not."

Relieved with this answer, Minitz closed the door and locked it behind him. A little while later, there were soft footsteps that I think neither Ivana nor Talia heard. David, it sounded like, had been sent to guard the room.

Chapter Sixteen

BUT IN THE morning, the merchant did not make any mention of the magic worked on his daughters. He seemed withdrawn and hardly spoke to Talia. Talia for her part clung to Ivana and was as quiet as I had ever seen her.

So I had more time, but how much more? A day? A week? It was impossible to know, and I could not live with the uncertainty of my fate. Better to be shattered than to live in a seesaw of hope. I would tell the truth at last. Perhaps I should have told it long before. Talia and Ivana were more likely to be overgenerous than under. But it had been easier to lie, and besides—I was used to it. The queen had taught me year after year. To unlearn it in a few weeks was a magic of its own, but a magic that did not come with any guarantees.

Talia and Ivana were reading together one night. They had long since finished the duke's letters and moved on to books. This one described a young noblewoman stealing some bit of vegetable root from a neighbor's garden. Ivana complained that no noblewoman would do such a thing.

"Why not?" asked Talia.

"Because they are never hungry," said Ivana.

"Just because they have sufficient to eat does not mean they are never hungry," I interjected.

Ivana was obviously puzzled, but it was Talia who asked, "What do you mean, Mirror?"

"Only that there are other kinds of hungers. Hunger for power, for love, for beauty. Hunger for anything that one does not already have. And it is the nobility in my experience who are most adamant about having what they wish. They have never learned to do without."

Even as I said this, I knew it was not really true of my sister. She had known what it was to do without, but at some point she had decided that it would never happen again, at any cost. What was interesting to me was that she never did find what she sought. The ultimate power she had over the king did not extend to his daughter. The beauty she twisted from so many deaths could never compare to a natural, untouched face. And love? Well, perhaps that was one hunger my sister had never felt.

"And how do you know so much about nobility?" Talia asked.

I gave the truth slowly. "The woman who owned me before was one of the nobility," I said.

"And she abandoned you in the forest?" It seemed Ivana had told Talia more about me than I had realized. "What had you done to her that she would throw away such a valuable source of magic?"

"She did not throw me away," I said stiffly.

"Then where is she?" asked Talia.

No reason not to be as blunt as Talia. "Dead," I said.

Talia stepped away from me. She held her hands out to Ivana, and they both had their backs to the door as they stared at me across the room. It was amusing, but not in a pleasant way. Had I been right to keep the truth from them? Well, it was too late now.

"You killed her?" whispered Ivana.

"No!" Did my voice make my ridicule clear? "She would never have given me a chance to kill her, I assure you."

"I don't believe you," said Talia. "Who was she?"

I said the truth because I was tired of always being the one to lie. "She was my sister."

There was a long silence then. I was grateful for that, at least. I felt as fragile as plain glass without any back to it. Even the smallest, high-pitched noise could have broken me.

"Your sister?" Ivana spoke very softly, in a low tone. I noticed that she did not hold herself quite as far away as she had. On the other hand, she did not come closer, either.

"Yes," I said.

"You are not a mirror, then?"

Which was a ridiculous question, but I suppose I had said too much already not to answer that. "Of course I am a mirror," I said. "Now. But I was not always a mirror."

"Your sister—was a witch?" asked Talia.

"Correct again," I said. "I was a witch also."

"But—how?" asked Ivana. "Why?"

"She took my magic and used it to trap me in this," I said. So few words, so much pain. "And then she used me to make herself beautiful for as long as I remained with her. Forever, or so she thought."

"What happened to her?" Talia again.

"I do not know. She came to me every day. And then she did not come anymore." No need to mention the prince and princess and the seven little men. They did not matter here.

"You never told me," said Ivana. "All this time, I thought you were a mirror. A magic mirror."

So it was she who discovered the betrayal first, not Talia, as I had expected. "I am sorry," I said.

"You are not," Talia threw at me. Immediately, she went to Ivana, put an arm around her shoulders and held her tightly.

I found I was not ready to give up. Not yet. "No, you are right. I am not sorry for what I did then. What did I know of you, Ivana? Only that you were a desperate peasant girl who might take me from my place on the wall and help me find magic. If I had told you the truth then, can you tell me honestly you would have acted no differently toward me?"

"I—I—" stuttered Ivana.

"No!" I said. "You would have run away from me the instant I told you the truth." And she would have been right to do so. "As for you," I said, turning my words to Talia, "if Ivana had not immediately elicited your sympathy with her false story of a father killed by bandits, would you have done anything more than offer her a few coins? More than enough for a peasant girl's needs, yes?"

I could see from the clear spots of red in Talia's cheeks that I had hit the mark there, but I found I was sorry for that too. I did not mean to drag Ivana into the mess, but I could not avoid it. The truth was, we had both been desperate to have what we wanted. We did not mind lying for it.

"Perhaps," said Talia, hardly moving her lips. She and Ivana stood apart now. "But afterward, in the inn—you could have told me then. I was willing."

"Yes, you were willing to be changed then. To take

my magic and Ivana's face—but not for our sakes. If we had told the truth then, would you have returned the favor? No. You would have kept Duke Fensky to yourself."

Talia sighed. She knew it was true. "So, we all lied," she said.

"We were all desperate," I said. "And we had no reason to trust one another."

"Until now," said Ivana.

"Yes, until now." I hoped. "And that is why I am asking you to help me."

"Help you? How?" asked Talia and Ivana at once.

"I need more magic." There, how much bolder could I be?

Talia stared at me, and I knew I was not quite forgiven, not yet. "The cook," she said. "That was not about getting more magic for Ivana, was it? It was about magic for you."

It had all been about magic for me. At least, I thought it had. At some point my motives may have changed, but I did not know when that exact moment was. Sometime in the last few weeks I had changed from the mirror I had been to a girl I had thought was longer dead even than my sister. A girl who could love and trust again.

"And the truth is," said Ivana, "she did help us.

Both of us. She saved me from my father."

"And me from mine," Talia put in.

"If not for her, I would be married to old Vanye, right now. If he had not beaten me to death already."

"Yes, but look on the bright side—your father would have had the horse he always wanted." It was a bleak humor, but that was the only kind I knew.

"And you, Talia. You would be marrying the duke now," said Ivana.

"More important than that, I would still be mooning after that idiot Blenin and hating my father and myself for not having him." There was a small, half-bitter smile on her lips.

"You see?" said Ivana. She reached out for me, and I felt her hand stroke my glass. There seemed to be a tenderness in it that I had never felt before.

"You are right." Talia sounded grudging. "You have helped us, even if it wasn't for our sakes."

"And perhaps it was," offered Ivana. "She could have chosen someone else, after all."

"In the forest?" I asked. I did not want to give myself credit I did not deserve.

"After the forest," said Ivana. "You could have remained in the inn. You could have changed the inn woman or anyone else there. You could have waited until we came here and found a servant to change. Or anyone.

It didn't have to be me. It didn't have to be Talia."

She was right! But I had never once thought of it. We had passed dozens and dozens of other choices, but I had stayed with Ivana. I must have become attached to her from the very first. And Talia too.

"It doesn't matter why she did it. We owe her a debt. And my family always pays its debts." There was a glint in Talia's eyes, as if daring me to tell her I wouldn't accept payment.

But the hope that rose inside me was too powerful for me to deny it. "Debts?" I asked hopefully.

"Yes," said Talia. "If you must have magic to become human again, I'll make sure we buy you magic. How much do you need?"

Magic was hardly something to be measured like a bolt of cloth or weighed like a crate of apples. It could not even be quantified in lives, for every life had more or less of it.

"How much can you give me?" I asked instead.

"Greedy mirror," scolded Talia.

If I were human, I might have blushed.

"Well, I don't know how much I will be able to wheedle out of Father," said Talia. "But I will get what I can."

"And then what?" asked Ivana.

"And then I'll teach you both how to bargain," said

Talia. "After all, if I am to truly be a merchant woman on my own, I will need a great deal more practice in the market here in town."

She made me almost believe she could do it, wherever we found the true witch.

Chapter Seventeen

IT WAS a simple task to arrange for a trip to the town after that. Talia managed to get a half dozen gold coins from Merchant Minitz, which would have been plenty a hundred years ago. I did not know about now. Was there more magic, to make it cheaper? Or less, to make it dearer?

I brooded as the girls prepared for the trip. It was not for myself that I worried now, but for Talia and Ivana. I had entangled them in this now and could not see how to get them out. Where I went, they would be with me. The dangers I faced, they would face as well. I tried to tell them of my concerns, but Talia would only wave a hand at me and tell me I sounded like I had grown as old as her father and as afraid of shadows. Ivana would only say, with a tear in her eye, that I deserved a chance.

The day of the journey had arrived. Talia and Ivana were filled with excitement about seeing the market and all its wonders. I could not help but feel a portion of the same. As the carriage drove onward, I sat quietly and felt the magic ahead of us grow stronger, and by some miracle, directly in front of us as we drove closer to town. I did not have to tell the carriage to turn away, for the witch I had come for was in the marketplace after all. Perhaps I had been wrong about her power, or her danger, I thought.

Then the carriage stopped and the door opened. If the sound of magic could have shattered my glass, this would have done it. If the heat of magic could have melted my glass, this would have done it. If the weight of magic could have crumbled my glass, this would have done it.

But as suddenly as I felt it, the magic disappeared, and I was left surrounded by only the overwhelming scent of humans in their worst state. Where was the magic I needed? I found I could not even sense a hedge witch here.

"Are you ready?" asked Talia.

"Yes," I said, forcing optimism to my voice. "I am ready."

Ivana stepped out, then reached back for me and tucked me into the waist of her simple gown. We moved out into the jostling swell of bodies. Talia put a cloth to her mouth, but Ivana was not bothered by any of it. No doubt she had smelled worse.

I noticed as we walked that the servant from the front

of the carriage followed behind us at some distance. The driver waited where we had left him, for our return.

We made our way past a fish market, then a cheap wooden stage where four dirty, awkward players were unbelievable as kings, let alone queens. There were several hundred people milling about, but few of them appeared to have money to buy. Most gawked, a few made raucous comments to all who passed them by.

I could smell the fish. I could smell the sweat and rotten fruit around the stage. I could smell the bright heat of the day. But of magic, I could neither smell nor taste nor see anything at all. And yet I enjoyed it all without a hint of fear. How long had it been since I had been entertained? How long since I had been out among people who did not fear me and hate me as much as my queen? How long since I had enjoyed simple fun with friends?

A few steps past the stage there were jugglers and beggars, hard to tell apart, for both wore torn, dirt-streaked clothes and held their hands out for anything offered. I wondered as Talia put a hand to her pocket to pass out a few smaller coins of her own, if the beggars' acts were as much a sham as the juggling. But I dared say nothing aloud for fear of drawing attention to myself. If they had a reason to look for me, I had no doubt there were dozens of pickpockets who could snatch me out of my hiding place in a moment.

And while I thought I had enough magic to protect myself from thieves, I would then be separated from Talia and Ivana. Even if I could start over again with another girl, I found I did not wish to. I had become attached to Talia and Ivana, and I did not want to give them up.

"Oh, look!" said Ivana, drawing me out of my own thoughts. She had found a stall with tiny creatures made of blown glass. A small brownish deer stood next to a family of rabbits leaping across the way. A glass tree towered above them all, to give the scene scale. And bits of green glass and sand had been scattered on the wooden floor to make it look like the undergrowth of a forest.

I was reminded of the time my sister had dared me to ride atop the back of a mother doe. It had been late summer, and early days yet, years before Zerba died. I waited under cover of a row of prickly bushes that I became far too well acquainted with that day. It was near dusk when I caught first sight of the doe with her swollen belly hanging low. My sister crouched next to me, making motions to urge me to go. But I waited until the doe was so close to the bushes I could feel her breath on my face.

Then I leaped, slung my right leg across her back and held tight to her neck. She bucked, but I used magic to hold tight. I was afraid for my life, if truth be known. The ride lasted for what seemed to be both minutes and hours. Too long and too short. The doe leaped over the stream and dragged my feet through the water. Then she brushed against trees to shake me off and finally began a headlong flight down a steep hill.

I caught a glint of metal in the field below us and could sense the magic-beckoning spell that surrounded it. In the instant before the doe stepped into it, I knew what it was. A bear trap. Then I heard the mechanism spring closed. It was several heartbeats later that the doe gave in to her pain. She fell over, trapping me in the process, though my leg was whole. I was very close to her as she let out her moan of farewell. It was a sound I can never forget, a long keening note that rose in the air and seemed to echo back at me a thousand times, chiding me for my foolishness.

I lay there under her cooling body until my sister arrived.

"Well, that was well done," she said. "A ride and a death." As though it had been my purpose to kill the doe.

She used magic to lift the doe's body enough so that I could scramble out. My leg was numb down to my toes and I stumbled trying to walk on it. My sister gave me a hand and helped me to a log.

"You didn't take her life to your magic," she said as she bent over the lifeless doe.

"No," I said. I hadn't thought of it. I was glad I hadn't. It was strangely horrifying to me that my sister had.

She put her hand out to the doe's swollen stomach.

"The fawn is still alive, though. Just." There was a look of hunger on her face, and I knew that she intended to take the magic of the fawn's death to herself.

"Stop!" I said.

She looked up at me in puzzlement. "But it would be wasted otherwise."

"Please," was all I could add. I knew it made little sense.

"You don't mean I should just let it die."

"No," I said, with a sudden idea. I put my hands on the doe's belly and cut it neatly open with my magic. The tiny fawn was nestled inside. At the sight of me—or perhaps it was only my smell he noticed, for his eyes were closed—he seemed to shrink back, as if preferring to stay inside.

I lifted him out and lay him on the ground.

"It's born too young," said my sister.

"Maybe not," I said, desperate.

But she was right. The fawn never opened his eyes. He never lumbered to his feet, as I had seen healthy fawns do. He simply shivered in the cool of the oncoming night.

"I will take his life now," said my sister, before the end.

And I did not stop her. As she took his life, the fawn looked very small and still and nearly transparent. Very like the glass figure that Ivana touched with one finger, afraid to break it if she held it in her hand.

"It is beautiful," said Talia.

The man who owned the stall came forward. "Only two silvers for the lot," he said, tempting Ivana.

Ivana looked at me and shook her head quietly. The man cursed under his breath and stared as Ivana and Talia moved away. But I was glad. Like the beauty of the doe, the beauty of the glass figures was not for taking. A memory could not be shattered, after all, as real glass could.

Chapter Eighteen

AFTER THE GLASS stall, I noticed a scent of sweet cakes, but I could not see where it was. Then Talia whispered, "A witch," and pointed at a stall that looked like it could belong to no one else. There were little bags of herbs and charms hung from the wood. I strained to sense the magic, to gauge its worth, but my senses were as numb as if I had been given pepper to breathe. I could tell nothing.

"Mirror?" asked Ivana.

I realized then I had still not told her my true name. Soon, I thought. When we get home. Before I use the magic.

As we walked around the stall, an old crone came to greet us.

"What can I get for you, pretty things?" she said to Ivana and Talia. She opened her mouth wide when she spoke, and I could not see a single tooth in her gums. The smell of her breath was powerful indeed, but more with garlic and onions than with magic.

"My sister is here to buy magic," said Talia, nudging at Ivana.

"Sister, eh?" said the crone, looking from the one to the other. "You don't look like sisters."

Ivana ignored the comment and moved on to her purpose. "How much magic can I buy with this?" she asked, holding out Merchant Minitz's handful of gold coins with no attempt to bargain.

Talia looked as chagrined as I felt at this lack of bargaining.

The crone smiled, as well she ought. "It all depends on what you need it for," she said.

It was not true, but I wondered if the crone knew it.

"Oh, the magic's not for me," said Ivana as the witch stared into her eyes.

"Who, then? Your father? Your mother? Your lover? Who, child? I must know who."

Again, the crone seemed to misunderstand the workings of magic, but I thought nothing of it.

"For this," said Ivana. And she held me up.

No! I wanted to shout as the witch took me out of Ivana's slippery grip. Then, her hands to mine, I was inside the witch's wards. I knew immediately then that she was no ordinary old crone interested in the sale of a charm or two. In her, I could feel the pulse of the great heart of magic I had long been moving toward.

"Pretty little mirror," she said. "I have been waiting for you since I had to hide myself at the first scent of you at market this morning." A drop of saliva dripped from her pointed chin onto my glass, smearing my image of her.

I wanted to call to Ivana to help me, but it was hopeless against a witch with this much magic. This was surely the end of me. I should have remained in the forest. I should have stayed with Talia in the merchant's safe house. I should have told Talia to spend all her coins on the glass animals. They would be worth far more than I when this was over.

Then by some miracle I felt Ivana's hands smoothing back over me, drawing me back into her warmth. The witch had let me go, but why?

"Perhaps we could make a trade, you and I," said the witch, as if the matter meant nothing to her. "This mirror for—whatever you'd like in my stall." She held out her hands, offering all the musty bottles and bits of wood around us.

"No, thank you," said Ivana.

"Well, then." The witch shrugged, as though leaving the choice entirely to Ivana. Then with her head bowed, she moved back to her stall.

"Don't trust her," I said in a voice meant only for Ivana. But I could see how the witch's back twitched at the sound. Now I had given myself away far worse than Ivana had. She knew I could speak. She would surely not give me up.

"Just a moment," said the witch, just as I feared. "I have what you want back here." The witch ducked low, then moved a crate out of the way. "Ah, here it is. Come." She motioned to Ivana.

I did not dare whisper my warnings of care again. I told myself it would not matter anyway. If the witch wanted me, she would have me, and nothing Ivana did or did not do would make any difference. But I thought that it was only me she wanted, for my magic. I did not think, as I should have, of the value of any human life to a witch.

"This is my basket of magic," said the witch as Ivana came closer, bringing me with her. "You have only to take hold of it and the magic will stream from it to you." Her voice was low and coarse, but there was something mesmerizing about it.

I looked into the basket. It was woven not with reeds, but with snakes. Living snakes, frozen in place.

"Go on," the witch beckoned. But she did not touch the basket herself. I wondered why.

Ivana reached to do as the witch bid.

"Don't do it!" I shouted. But I was too late.

Ivana was frozen in place. Her hands gripped the sides of the basket as though holding to life itself, and her eyes were strangely closed.

"Ivana?" asked Talia, worried. "Mirror?"

"Stay away!" I warned.

But brave, impulsive Talia reached out her hand. And then she was as silent and frozen as her sister. Both were under the spell of the basket, along with all the others to whom the witch had pretended to offer magic. The basket had told them all a story that convinced them they should wish for death. And then the witch gathered them in for her own use and held them there.

There was a woman who was plunging a knife into her heart, for she had heard only then of her son's death. A man who killed the woman he loved and then tried to kill himself. A girl who had got a child in her belly she knew not how, and was strangling herself in despair.

A king. A merchant. A duke. A peasant. A woodsman. A hunter. A gypsy. A slave. A bandit. An actress. A servant. A sheriff. They had long been separated from their bodies, but they were none of them quite dead. If they were, then the witch would not be able to continually harvest their lives for her magic.

And so it would be for Ivana and Talia. I did not have the power to save them. I could only listen with a sinking heart as Ivana and Talia reacted to the horror the witch had prepared especially for them.

"Father! Oh, my dearest father," said Ivana. "How could she do this to you?"

"You stole him!" Talia shouted. "But that was not enough for you, was it? You had to kill him too." Talia's legs pumped in a panicked attempt to move forward, but her hands were still holding fast to the basket.

The witch seemed to have made sure that no one passing by could see any part of her stall. I could feel the cloak of her magic settle around us. We could expect no help from strangers, or even from the servant who was to be our guard. If he even knew we were missing, he would have no way to find us.

"Look at him, bleeding while you hold a knife," Ivana said, weeping.

"You are no sister to me," said Talia.

I could feel their desire to die, but I did not feel it myself. Perhaps it was because I was not holding to the basket. Or perhaps it was because I was a mirror and the witch had made the basket as a trap for humans only. It might have been the one time in my long life when it was better to be a mirror than a human, for my mind was clear as glass.

"No!" I cried. "Talia, Ivana, stop!"

Ivana trembled.

Did she hear me? I had to believe that she did, even inside this horrible basket. I was familiar to her.

"Remember the witch. Remember the basket," I said. I looked up to see the witch. Would she stop me? Her eyes glittered, but she made no move to take me away. Was she afraid of being trapped by her own magic? Or was she so sure of herself that it was all part of the spectacle to her?

Ivana took a sudden sharp breath, and I hoped that was a sign of some remaining consciousness.

"We were in the marketplace, in town. You touched the basket and the magic took you. Think. Open your eyes. Breathe deeply." I did not know if any of this would help, but I had to try something. I had no magic against the witch.

But as Ivana pondered this, Talia started up again.

"I can see him," she whimpered. "My dearest father. His head was broken by an axe, and she wielded it." She nodded at Ivana.

"It is not Ivana you see," I said calmly but as loudly as I could in the cacophony of dying. "It is a picture of her. An image made of magic. It is not real."

"It seems real," said Talia.

What could I say to make her believe? I could think only of the growing trust between the two sisters. After all that had passed between them by now, Talia would want to believe in Ivana.

"You know Ivana," I said. "You know she would not do this. She loves your father. She loves you too."

Talia's mouth opened. Her eyes blinked. I hoped she was beginning to break away from the spell, for I had to turn to Ivana next.

"The witch," I said. "Ivana, remember the witch."

Ivana's mouth opened. She breathed deeply—surely a breath of truth.

But then I heard the whisper of the witch. "Little mirror." Her fingers twitched, but she did not touch me. "I warn you," she said. "If you do not cease at once I will take my revenge out on you." But she sent no magic at me. The basket in a strange way protected me, for the witch did not dare touch it.

"Ivana," I said. "It is not your father there. It is only the workings of the witch's magic. She plays upon your worst fears, your darkest moments. She makes you see what you hope most not to see." And so it must have been with all the others whose lives I felt with us.

"But he is there," said Ivana tearfully.

I was firm. "No, he is not. Merchant Minitz is not with us at the market. It is only you and me and Talia, your sister."

Now Talia added her voice to mine. She had removed her hands from the basket. I could feel the power of the basket's magic begin to wane, as the flow of it was stopped on one side.

"Ivana, I am here," said Talia. "Let go of the basket. Let go of the vision."

There was a long moment in which the voices inside the basket seemed to grow louder. Ivana's face went white and she bit at her tongue until her mouth dripped blood. With a gasp, Ivana wrenched away from the basket.

Suddenly the dead voices were silenced. I could hear only heavy breathing around me from them, and the witch's voice rising in fury.

"Impossible," she raged. "Impossible."

I should have been afraid of her now. But I felt a ringing inside me, as though I had been filled with water and touched with a metal spoon. I had magic again. In stepping back from the basket, I had taken with me a portion of what it held.

Was it enough? I would have to wait to see.

"How did you do it?" demanded the witch.

"Miss Talia? Miss Ivana?" Merchant Minitz's servant called, and I realized then that the spell that had kept us from his view must have been broken.

There was a long moment as the witch seemed to be considering who of all those before her was worth an effort to keep, if any of us at all.

Then Ivana and Talia ran toward the servant. I was jolted along with them, but only for a few steps. After that, I was flying to the witch like a bird with eager wings.

Ivana stretched her arms out for me, but I was far beyond her grasp. I tried to struggle away, to use my magic to change myself. But it was useless. The magic that I had taken from the basket was nothing in comparison to what the witch still maintained inside herself. I was trapped.

"Ah," said the witch, looking at her fearsome face in my glass. "Made for beauty, aren't you? Well, give some to me."

She wanted beauty? I would give her beauty! I thought of the most beautiful face I knew, and the one I hated above all. Then I cut away the flesh that hung from the witch's chin. I lightened the effect of the heavy brows, which seemed to take over her face. I chiseled at the cheekbones until they were delicate as ice. On and on I worked. Her hair, her hands, her crooked back—all became as my sister had been, the last I had seen her.

It was a perfect transformation. So perfect, in fact, that I stared at her, wondering—could it be? After a hundred years could my sister still be alive? It made no sense, for my sister would have come back for me, if she lived. She would not have given up her kingdom so easily. She would not have turned herself into this hideous reflection of herself. And she would have remembered me.

The witch's now tiny brows arched as she peered down at me. Her lips were pressed gently together, closing over perfect teeth. "Pretty little mirror, I wonder who made you." She turned me over in her hands and traced a line in my wood with a fingertip. "I do not know any witches who have the power for something like this."

I heard her voice like an echo in my glass. Was it the same voice as my sister's? Or had I made it the same?

"I cannot tell how old you are, or where you came from. Well, I will find out in time." She turned me back around and breathed to cloud my glass. Then she took a corner of her ragged dress and wiped at me.

My sister would not have been caught dead in such a dress. I felt a moment's relief at this proof that I was wrong. Stupid of me, to make this witch look like my sister, but I could undo it, someday. After all, it appeared that I would be with this witch for a very long time.

Suddenly, there was a rushing sound and then I felt a hand on my wood. A soft hand.

"Give my sister back her mirror."

It took me a moment to place the voice. But as soon as I looked up, I could see that Talia and Ivana waited still, refusing to heed the beckoning of the frightened servant beyond them as he held open the carriage door.

The witch smiled at the two girls. It was a beautiful smile—now that I had made it so. "I do not think I will. You, neither of you, know what to do with magic such as this."

It was a dismissal, and the witch did not think any

more than that was necessary. Why should she? Even I expected Ivana and Talia to leave me. But they did not.

And Talia found a stone on the ground and raised it. "I will destroy your basket," she threatened.

"Ha!" said the witch. "As if that could hurt my basket."

If she had not been so sure of herself. If she had kept silent . . .

Talia's raised hand moved an inch, to aim at the witch's face instead of the basket. There was no magic in the throw, but it landed as perfectly as if Talia had killed to succeed.

There was a cry when the stone struck the witch's left eye. Blood dripped onto my glass. I felt the tremble of angry magic all around me. Then the witch dropped me to clutch at herself, and Ivana leaped forward to catch me. A moment after that, we were all in the carriage, riding for home.

Chapter Nineteen

I THOUGHT AT first the witch would be quick to come after me. But days passed and there was no sign of her. I began to hope again. The world seemed to hope with me. Summer stayed late, and the yard outside Merchant Minitz's house hung on to life in bright fuchsias and purples and crimson. I hung to life too, enjoying every moment of freedom, afraid to be thought greedy in asking for more.

I did not care anymore about my form. Ivana and Talia treated me with more humanity than ever my sister had, and I loved them too much to drag them into more danger. So I told them not to worry, that there would be chances enough for magic for me when Ivana was married to Duke Fensky, and when Talia was a wealthy merchant. I said it for their sakes, though, not for mine.

I thought of a woman in my old forest village who

had two daughters. How I had hated those two. They teased and mocked me whenever I came out of the forest. And one night I snuck back to their home with them after dark. I listened at a crack in the door as their mother scolded them for being dirty. There was no anger in her voice, though. And when she served dinner, the girls complained there was not enough.

"I will get more for you," she said.

I could hear dishes scraped, and the girls did not complain again. The mother sat by their bedside and sang to them that night, a beautiful song about a princess with long hair who was trapped in a tower by an evil witch. She had to wait to be saved, but as she waited she sang the very song the mother sang to her daughters.

I think the daughters fell asleep long before I did. I listened outside the door until I could hear the woman snoring as well. And even after that, it took me hours to go back to the cold forest. And I returned night after night to hear that same song.

Until the night came that the mother's song ended early, on an unfinished note. I peeked into the house to see what was wrong and saw that she had fallen to the floor. Thinking only to help her, I rushed in, heedless of the noise I made.

She was too dead for me to take her magic. She must have been dying for a long time and no one noticed.

The girls had leaped out of their beds, screaming that the witch had killed their mother. But I felt silence inside my heart and stared at the dinner table, where there were only two bowls this night.

The mother had given her food to her girls night after night, and she had done it gladly. I slipped away, ducking away from the crockery thrown badly and the curses. I told Zerba about the mother, and she said only that the woman would be sad not to be able to give to her daughters anymore.

I had always thought it a strange thing to say, and had wondered if Zerba had meant something about her own death, which came only a few months after that. But I had never felt anything akin to that love before now, before Talia and Ivana. They were at least as much my daughters as ever the queen was my sister. And if my remaining a mirror was the food they needed to live, I was glad to give it to them.

And so it was that I watched them at night, feeding on the love they showed each other, on the simple moments of peace they had together, and I did not ask them to think of me or my needs. They did not mean to forget me, and I did not blame them for having their own lives. It was what I wished most for them.

It was enough for me to watch Ivana write letters to Fensky, though she feared to send them. Talia tried to convince her to do so, but Ivana would always find one reason or another that the letter she had just written was not good enough. She was afraid that Fensky would see through her to her true identity.

"Does it matter, really?" asked Talia once in the middle of a dark night when the beginnings of a violent summer storm tried to break the window glass and get inside.

"Does it matter?" echoed Ivana. Her face went red, then purple.

"Yes. You are who you are, no matter what face you wear, surely."

Ivana considered it for a moment. I think I understood how she felt. I had been a mirror for so long that there were times I could not remember what it was like to be human. Perhaps that was another reason why I was content to remain as I was. It would be far more difficult to learn to feel, taste, touch, smell, and hear as a human, with all of a human's frailties.

If either girl had asked me, I would have changed them then. But they did not ask. They too were afraid of change.

"Promise me you will not tell him," said Ivana in a hoarse, desperate voice.

"All right." Talia shrugged, holding up her hands. "I promise." A burst of thunder from the first storm of fall punctuated her words.

Ivana hardly heard it. "Promise me you won't tell your father, either," Ivana insisted.

"I won't tell him." But it sounded as though Talia had lost her fear that Minitz would force her into a marriage with Fensky. I had heard several discussions over the dinner table about the merchant's next trading journey, after the wedding. Talia proved how apt she was to be at Minitz's side, and Blenin was not mentioned.

"Promise, too, you won't tell Silva or the other servants," said Ivana.

"I—" Talia began.

"Or anyone else in the world," Ivana went on, in a panic.

Talia sighed and put her hands on Ivana's shoulders. "I promise," she said. "Is that good enough?"

Ivana looked down. The fear was still in her stiff stance.

"You are safe," said Talia. "And I think you are happy, aren't you?"

Ivana nodded, and began to weep.

"What?" Talia asked. "What is it?"

"I am too happy," said Ivana, through hiccoughs. "I am too safe. I feel like this must be a dream." She patted at her face and looked into my glass—several feet away on the dresser—once more. "It must be a dream. Where else is there magic such as this but in a dream?"

"If it is a dream," said Talia, "then you know where to find me when you wake. Come and I will be your sister no matter what face I wear."

"Truly?" asked Ivana, her eyes shining but no longer tearful.

"Of course truly. If you ask me, the most magic thing about this mirror of yours is that it brought us together, where we should have been to begin with, where we will always be forever more."

Ivana sighed, content once more.

Was it possible that some things were destined to be? And if so, were my sister and I meant to be together, with or without magic, as Talia and Ivana thought they were?

"I love you," said Talia, for the first time.

"I love you too," said Ivana.

I wanted to chime in that I loved them both as well, but it was not my place. Not then, perhaps not ever. A mother does not need to say her love. She shows it, sometimes by being silent while others find their words.

Finally, the day came when Merchant Minitz announced it was time to visit Duke Fensky, as final preparations for the wedding were in place. Talia was calm, but Ivana grew even more distraught. She seemed to hardly move. Certainly she was incapable of making the multitude of choices that Talia seemed to think necessary for a bride meeting her future husband.

"What will you wear to dinner the first night?" asked Talia one morning. She held out Ivana's pale yellow gown. "This one?" She took out the pink. "Or this one?" She shook her head and searched for the water blue silk. "This one, perhaps?"

"I have no opinion. You choose." Ivana waved her hand and moved to the bed to sit. She put her head down and stroked at her temples.

"You are afraid of the duke," guessed Talia.

"Afraid of myself," said Ivana. "Afraid that he will see through me."

Talia knelt down beside the bed and looked up at Ivana. "You will charm him," she said. "I am sure of it. If ever there was a woman for the man who wrote those letters, it is you."

"Do you mean it?" Ivana's head lifted an inch.

"Of course I do. I would never lie to my sister."

The sincerity in Talia's voice was too much. A memory overtook me. I thought of the day my sister and I were sent out to catch dinner in the forest. Zerba suggested a pheasant or perhaps a wild boar, but it was a dismal day to be out. Winter whispered at us in the cold air and the grim clouds above our heads.

I went to all my best places for pheasants, but I found not a one. My sister tried her special calls for the boars, but none appeared. I began to look for fish in the stream, but the ones I saw swam too fast for me to catch with my hands, and even those would have made a skimpy meal for three.

"We'll have to go home," said my sister, when it grew dark.

"Without dinner?" I knew Zerba would scold us. My sister might have more magic, but no one could beat Zerba when it came to sheer volume of displeasure.

My sister shrugged. "You want to keep going? In the dark?"

"Might as well," I said. I began to use magic then. I knew that without it I had no hope of finding anything. I had always been so clumsy, with my big feet and tall shoulders. If I expected to surprise an animal, I'd need more than my own bare skills.

We went south, away from the village, into the darkest parts of the forest. I saw empty nests and empty dens. I heard animals in the distance. But there were none anywhere near me.

I called for a rest. We sat on a moss-covered boulder, and my sister brushed herself clean. I watched her, and my suspicions mounted.

"You're doing this," I said. "Aren't you?"

"Doing what?" she asked, all innocence.

"You're keeping the animals away."

"How would I do that?"

"I don't know." It made no sense. But I knew the taste of my sister's magic, and it was all around. "You're using magic for it."

"Why would I use magic to keep our dinner away? Don't you think I am as hungry as you are?"

"You are lying," I insisted.

"I would never lie to my sister," she said. As sincerely as Talia had said it to Ivana.

And because I had no answer to that, we got up and went on our way again. Not long afterward, I fell over a log I had been sure was not in my way until my sister put it there. As I lay clutching my bleeding knee, I wondered why my sister, who had been cruel to others, now was cruel to me as well.

"Are you ready to go home now?" she asked after holding a clean corner of her dress against my wound. "Ready to tell Zerba we have no dinner for her?"

Was that why she was doing this? To make me go home and face Zerba's wrath? Well, I did not intend to let her have her way.

"No," I said. Next, I stumbled into the stream and nearly drowned, fell into a mole's hole, walked into a tree branch that almost blinded me, and was pecked to bleeding by a swooping hawk.

At last, I gave in. "All right," I said, exhausted. "Let's go home."

"If you're sure," said my sister.

I bowed my head, and now, of course, we moved without mishap and made our way back to the clearing by Zerba's hut in no time.

I slumped against the doorway.

"Is that you, Mira?" asked Zerba.

"It's me," I said.

"Come in, then. I didn't mean for you to spend so long out there."

I opened the door and looked in. My mouth was open, ready to explain about our lack of success at finding dinner. But I was too stunned at what I saw to say anything at all.

The hut was as light as full day, and warm with magic. Steaming food was set on the table in front of us, not only wild boar, but chicken and beef as well. And buttered squash, and peas and sweet cakes and honeycomb. And wine. My first wine.

"Why?" was all I could get out.

"It's your birthday," said my sister, from behind me.

"My birthday? What do you mean?" I had been born in the spring, or so my mother told me. She certainly never celebrated my birth.

"It has been one year since you became an apprentice to Zerba," she said.

I had never thought of it as a birthday, but in some

sense, I suppose it was. I was astonished that anyone had thought to celebrate it.

"Your sister reminded me," said Zerba. "And offered to add a little magic for the feast." She waved her hand at the lights, which were my sister's signature rose color.

I turned to my sister. "You! Why didn't you say anything? Why did you torment me so?"

"I wanted to be sure it was a surprise," said my sister.

Well, it had certainly been a surprise. I felt sore all over—and I was not completely sure that the food before us would make up for it.

I looked at my sister, and she laughed at me. "I would never lie to my sister," she said. "I did enjoy it. The most fun I've had all year." She held out her hand and drew me into the room. The smells were overwhelming after our long night of hopeless hunting. After I ate so much I could not stand, I laughed until I cried as my sister regaled Zerba with stories of the night's misadventures.

My sister had loved me then, as much as Talia loved Ivana. But if we had not been brought together by magic, I think that magic still would have come between us in the end. I vowed to myself then that I would not let the same thing happen to Ivana and Talia. If the witch from the marketplace found me again and demanded I go with her, I would agree without an argument. And Talia and Ivana would be better off without me, so long as the witch had no reason to look for them again.

Ivana stood, still looking fragile and unsure in front of the larger mirror. Finally, she nodded. "The blue," she said.

"Good," said Talia. "You won't regret it. Trust me. The duke will be enchanted with the blue."

"But will he be enchanted with me?" asked Ivana.

"Of course he will. Believe me, Ivana. I would never lie to my sister."

Chapter Twenty

THE FIRST DAY of the journey was full of sidelong glances between the two girls and strained, though effusive, conversation. The merchant heard Talia's superficial opinions on the colors of the turning leaves, the smell of fall in the air, the hope for crisp apples and cider, and on and on. Ivana chimed in about the coming harvest, a subject she knew much about. And the merchant listened with as much contentment as did I.

"My two daughters," sighed Merchant Minitz as we began the second day of the journey. He had just finished an enormous breakfast at a very fine inn on the way south, and if his stomach was larger, so was his pride and goodwill.

They had brought me along because Ivana said she wanted something familiar with her when she met the duke. I was warmed by the gesture. But then again, Ivana had always treated me with far more courtesy than I deserved.

Minitz nodded to the driver atop the carriage, tucked himself inside as the horses moved forward smoothly. They were not as formidable as the ones on the wagon, but they certainly stepped with more style.

"How are you this morning?" Merchant Minitz looked at Ivana, whose hands were twisting over themselves.

"I am well, Father." She had not been this way yesterday, but we were drawing ever closer to our destination.

"You are nervous," said Minitz. "About meeting Duke Fensky for the first time."

"As well she should be," said Talia. "How many times have I heard you say it is not proper for a girl to be eager for marriage?"

Minitz turned slowly, and I think only I saw the narrowing of his eyes that warned danger. "I said that?" he asked.

"Yes. You said that a marriage is the most important moment in a girl's life, for it binds her to another before earth and heaven, for good or ill," continued Talia. "So why should she not be nervous?"

I had never heard the merchant say such a thing to Talia. It could have been during one of those times I was left in the room. But I guessed it was something he had said even before Ivana and I had come into his life, and Talia did not realize it. She was speaking as herself, because she had become so used to her new face she did not think to guard herself against slips such as this one.

Merchant Minitz pointed a finger at Talia. "I said that to Talia," he said. "Not to you, *Ivana.*"

Too late, Talia realized what she had done. She blanched.

"You are not Ivana, are you?" asked Merchant Minitz in a cold voice I had not heard since that night on the road when he first saw Ivana before his wagon.

"Wh—what makes you say that?" Talia stuttered. It was not planned, but nothing could have made Talia sound less like herself and more like Ivana.

Merchant Minitz, seeking confirmation, turned to Ivana. "And you are not Talia, are you?"

I hoped against hope that the deception would stand one more day, but Ivana took one look at Merchant Minitz and began to shake her head. "I am sorry, so sorry," she said.

The game was over.

"How?" demanded Minitz.

Ivana gestured to me. "It was the mirror, the magic mirror."

I did not defend myself.

Minitz reached forward across the carriage, and I wondered if this would be the end of me. I almost regretted it, for what good would my death do for Ivana and Talia now? But Minitz's hand shook, then clenched into a fist. He slammed it into the open palm of his other hand and sat back down, eyes flickering in Talia's direction.

"Tell me why," Merchant Minitz demanded. Of Talia, not of Ivana. He clearly did not believe Ivana was capable of engineering this debacle.

"I wanted Blenin," said Talia. Wanted, past tense.

"You wanted him so much that you would give away your whole self? Your mother's face? Her figure? Everything I loved about her?" Merchant Minitz was suddenly teary-eyed. He seemed to have aged ten years in the last moment, without any magic.

"I am not my mother," said Talia defiantly. "And I have the right to my own life."

"I see you have done so well with it already," said Minitz.

The words cut through Talia's strength. "I didn't know," she said. "I was in love with him."

"With his face perhaps," said Minitz. "And you did not see past that. But I did. I told you he was no better than a thief, and you did not believe me."

"I believe you now," said Talia, hanging her head.

"Too late," said Minitz bitterly.

"No, it is not too late," said Ivana. "There is no

reason why the mirror cannot change us back."

"Oh?" Minitz's face changed entirely, from despair to hope.

"No!" said Talia. Her head came up. "I mean, Father—please."

"But why not? I thought you agreed with me that you should not choose your own husband. The duke is a good man. You cannot hope for a better marriage, in position, in wealth, or in honor." It sounded to me as though Minitz had said these words before, to convince Talia to marry the duke the first time. But they did not work twice.

"Father, in this face or in my old face, I will not marry the duke. Not unless you force me to it."

I wondered why she did not tell him of her plan to become a merchant woman. It might have flattered him, but it seemed she was too proud to try to sweeten her refusal.

"Must I force you to do what I think best?" asked Merchant Minitz.

Talia put a hand to her chin, as though she had to force it to shake from side to side. Her mouth opened to speak no, but there was no sound to it. "Father," she added later, as a whisper.

Merchant Minitz sighed. "Good," he said, and turned to Ivana, who was fully expecting to be treated as she had always been treated by those who knew who she truly was.

"You may leave me here, if you wish," she said, pointing out the window of the carriage.

For the first time, I noticed the countryside we were moving toward. It was hilly, and the sky above it had turned gray with dusk. Not far away a forest loomed, a familiar little stream running through it. I could hear the tinkling sound of the water against the rocks.

"This is very near my village. I never should have left it. I never should have believed I could have more."

"You are not a merchant's daughter," said Minitz as he looked out into a passing village. I did not know if it was Ivana's or just one very like hers, but there were dirty men sitting outside dirty huts. Children crying. Fields in need of tilling. Huts in need of mending.

"No," said Ivana, staring out at the dismal scene. "My father is a peasant farmer, and not a very good one at that."

"You found this mirror and left him. Then you found our wagon on the road." He did not have the events in the right order, but it was close enough.

"Yes," said Ivana. She moved toward the door of the carriage, as though she were ready to jump out if she had to, if Merchant Minitz told her he had not even the time to stop the carriage that long.

"Father, you cannot send her back to him," said Talia.

"And why not? Because he arranged a marriage for her

that she found unacceptable? And instead of telling him her concerns, she simply fled them and remade herself so that he would never see her again?"

If he had thought carefully, he'd have known this was not true. It was not in keeping with Ivana's character to rebel against a reasonable father's choice for a husband.

"He beat her!" I said, because someone had to say it.

Minitz started. His eyes darted around the carriage. "Who said that?" he asked.

"I said it. The mirror."

He picked me up, but this time his hands were trembling with fear and his fingers ran across the delicate seams between my glass and wood. "The magic mirror speaks, as well?" he asked.

"Obviously," I said.

He jumped in astonishment, then set me back down carefully, as gingerly as if he were holding a scorpion in his hands. And just as well, for if I could speak and change faces, how could he know what else I could do?

It was tempting for a moment to turn him into an ass, for that was what he was. I could see clearly the way his face would lengthen and his ears grow furry and taller on the side of his head. His stomach would still hang down, though. He would be as gluttonous and stupid as ever.

Or perhaps I should have been kinder to him. He had been largely good to Ivana. But I had thought he had come to love her as he loved Talia. I thought he was as much a father to them as I was a mother, and to realize that he was not made me angry. A protective instinct I had never felt before was roused, and it was hot as any of my sister's fiery magic. Yet I did not need magic to chastise him.

"If you knew anything about Ivana, you would know that she has offered you the love her own father never deserved. But perhaps you are no better than he. Do you beat your daughter as well?" In my day, there were many parents proud to beat their children for their own good. But Minitz was obviously a different sort.

"I am not a child beater," said Minitz. His eyes went wide and his face went pale.

"And he would have married her to an old man who would beat her yet more. All because her father wanted the old man's horse, and to be free of the cost of feeding his own child."

"Is this true?" Minitz demanded of Ivana.

She was weeping. "Yes, Fa—" she began, but could not continue.

Minitz stared at me, and I wondered what more I could say on Ivana's behalf. Should I take the blame for the plan to deceive him? Should I tell him that Ivana had argued against me, that she had never wanted it? Or would that only enrage him further?

Then suddenly he jumped to his feet. "Stop the carriage!" he shouted loud enough that the whole world might have heard him.

The driver certainly did, for the horses slowed instantly. But it was not fast enough for Merchant Minitz. He had to pound on the roof and repeat himself. His mouth had drawn back against his teeth, and there was color high in his cheeks.

I stared at him in astonishment. This was the Minitz I had feared all along, the one who discovered how he had been tricked.

The horses still moving, Merchant Minitz was reaching for the door, pushing Ivana out in front of him. Once he had leaped out, he stared about him in fury, then turned to Ivana. "Is this your village?" he demanded.

A few villagers had gathered to gawk at the sight of a merchant and his daughter arguing. Through the open door of the carriage, I saw a few sly grins and nudging whispers. They seemed to think it amusing that the middle class had no better manners with family than did the lower.

Ivana looked around her. One village here in the north must look very much like another. And she had not been here for several months—a lifetime of experience to her. It might take her time to tell if this was home.

But slowly, her eyes glazed over, and she shook her head. "It is not. But it does not matter. Leave me here. I will find my way home somehow."

Merchant Minitz grabbed Ivana by the arm and shook her. “You are not protecting him from me, are you?” His voice was a roar.

“I—I—please, please, don’t hurt me.” Ivana, misunderstanding the anger, put her hands over her head and knelt down in the dirt, prostrate, ready for another beating.

The tableau held for a moment. Angry merchant, cowed daughter. Then Merchant Minitz realized what he had done. He took a sharp breath then gently bent toward Ivana and lifted her up.

“It is not you I mean to hurt,” he said softly. “It is a man who would beat his daughter. A man like that is no father at all and has no place on this earth.”

Ivana’s face was blank.

Talia, who had held me up so that I could witness all this, whispered to her, “Ivana. Look at him.”

Ivana shook like an old woman, but she lifted her head and stared into Minitz’s eyes. If she did not understand his words, there was no mistaking the meaning of the love in his eyes.

He held out his arms and took a step forward. Ivana took the other step to close the distance. Then the merchant hugged her so tightly that I feared her ribs would break. There was a sound of a crack and I thought for a moment I was right. But it was only a stone thrown by one of the village boys, who apparently wished for more of an end to this show.

Minitz cursed under his breath, then cursed louder at the villagers still watching the scene. He helped Ivana into the carriage gently, then slammed the door shut and shouted at the driver again. "Go on!"

The horses gained speed quickly and soon the village was far behind us.

"You are my daughters," Merchant Minitz said slowly. "Both of you. Never doubt it. I do not."

The words seemed to fill the carriage so that there was no place for anything else, fear or relief. Only the warmth of love everywhere except in me. For I was no longer needed here. These daughters had a father, and a better one than ever a mirror would be. I had thought to satisfy my old wish for humanity with them, but now it throbbed in me again.

And with it came the taunt of magic ahead, deep, dangerous, dark magic, as thick and delicious as any I had ever tasted before. The magic of the witch at the market, who had not come in search of me after all. She had not had to. It seemed I had come instead to her.

Was it destiny or just bad luck? It did not matter. I had lost the chance for love. Now I would have the chance for magic instead.

When night came, the carriage went on and the horses followed the road by moonlight.

"What about Duke Fensky?" Talia asked much later, when Ivana had fallen mercifully asleep.

Merchant Minitz waved a hand. "I will decide about Duke Fensky when I decide," he said.

The road ended as a massive edifice of gray stone rose before us, clearly outlined in torchlight. It was time for us all to decide.

Chapter Twenty-One

TWO SERVANTS dressed in fine silver and brown livery appeared, taking hold of the reins and leading the horses to the stables.

"Duke Fensky." Merchant Minitz bowed at a finely dressed man with a wide mustache.

The man shook his head. "I am but his servant. The duke awaits you within." He waved to the drawbridge.

Merchant Minitz shrugged off his embarrassment at mistaking the man he had seen but once before. Then Minitz nodded to Talia and Ivana and offered each an arm as he led onward. Once the drawbridge had closed behind us, the dank smell clung to us as Ivana clung to Merchant Minitz.

The servant stopped in front of a huge oak door and pushed with all his strength against it. A large, hooded man stood before us when the door opened.

The servant bowed. "Duke Fensky," he said reverently and moved away.

"Come." Fensky's voice boomed at us, and there was a deep intelligence in it that made me wonder what could be wrong with him. He was not hunchbacked, which I had half expected, and if his mind was not deficient, why would he ask a merchant's daughter to marry him?

"Duke Fensky." The merchant came closer and put out his hand.

The duke shook it heartily.

Merchant Minitz tried to lean forward, so as to look beneath the hood. But as soon as the duke saw the movement, he stepped to the side and stared at Ivana and Talia. I was not surprised by his interest in them, but it was his subsequent examination of me I found odd. Did he sense I was magic? But if he knew that much about magic, surely he would have his own, and I sensed none in him.

"Which is Talia?" he asked, turning away from me.

Talia swallowed in fear, but Merchant Minitz did not hesitate. "Here she is," he said, pointing to Ivana.

"Yes," said the duke, nodding his hood slowly. "I had thought so." He stared at her, and somehow I had the sense that he could see within her, to the real Ivana.

"I can see in your eyes that only you could be the girl I wrote my letters to."

It could easily have been a ridiculous thing to say, but somehow it was not. Instead it seemed honest and wonderful. Finally, the duke turned to Talia. "And you are the beautiful Ivana, yes?"

Talia nodded, relieved.

"Your new father has written to me about you. I am pleased to meet you." Fensky stared at her. Why? If the merchant had told the story of Ivana's professed history, perhaps there were signs of grief he was looking for and not finding. Or did he sense the taste of magic in her, and in Ivana, as he did in me?

Talia curtsied. Ivana did the same, though perhaps not as gracefully. The duke, however, showed no sign of suspicion at the slightly awkward movement. Perhaps he thought it was only nerves. Perhaps it was.

"I am sure you need to rest after your long journey. Come, I will show you to your rooms and send for you when it is time for dinner," said Fensky, and he led us through the grand entrance into the great room.

I noticed that the curtains over the vista were gold and white and looked ancient, and for some reason I remembered the queen telling me of the curtains in her castle, that they were gold and white. But she had never taken me to the castle. I do not know why.

I was turned to the side and saw two great walnut wood chairs, intricately carved, standing on either side of the staircase. Those could have been the queen's as well. They were her dark, heavy style. But when I quested toward them, they had no scent of magic. In fact, they were as clean of magic as everything else in the duke's home, strangely clean, as though no creature had ever died here and left its power behind.

Yet the dark magic was not far away. It was a strange combination of magic and unmagic that swirled together here, and I wondered what would become of it all. I wanted to believe that all would be well with Ivana and Talia, that they would have rich, fulfilling lives of their own choosing. Unlike mine. And my sister's, come to think of it. For all her power and ambition, I think she had been as unhappy as I had been. There could never be enough magic to get her what she wanted. Maybe it was because she didn't know what she wanted.

Ah, well. That time was passed. There was no getting for either of us what we wanted now.

Ivana and Talia were given adjoining rooms, and Talia passed me to Ivana. Not long after the duke said his farewells to Ivana, Talia knocked on her door and peeked her head in. "It's a cavern in here too?" she asked, her voice echoing in the vastness of the cold stone walls and floors. There were rich tapestries hung without sparing, but I did not think a houseful of furniture could have filled this room.

"Well, a man like the duke wouldn't be satisfied with an ordinary house," said Ivana.

"Ohhh," said Talia. She came closer to Ivana and lifted her chin. "Is that the way it is with you then? Already? You've only just met the man, you know."

"It doesn't feel like I've just met him," said Ivana. She hugged herself against the cold of the room and swirled around, breathing as deeply as if she were in a field of flowers.

I felt my glass beginning to fog up with the chill.

"All those letters," Ivana went on. "I feel I couldn't know him any better if I'd spent a hundred years with him."

It was the kind of thing only youth would say, who had no idea of the real length of time. To spend a hundred years with someone, anyone, would be enough to show a hundred flaws.

"You didn't think his hood odd?" asked Talia.

Ivana shrugged. "If he is a bit shy, why not? He has the right to keep his privacy to himself. And I'm sure he will show himself to me when he feels he is ready."

"Hmmm," said Talia. She tried out Ivana's bed, sitting down on the corner as she had so often done back in Minitz's house. But this bed sank down immediately, and she found herself drowning in a soup of feathers.

Ivana helped her out, and the muffled squawks for help ceased.

Talia pulled away from Ivana and the bed and stood by the window. It was as if something had suddenly stepped between the two of them. "Well, I wish you all happiness with him," said Talia.

"Do you?" asked Ivana.

"What is that supposed to mean?" demanded Talia.

"Only that I wonder if you are regretting your choice, after all. The duke must look far more tempting now than he did in his letters. And in comparison to Blenin . . ."

"I told you already that I don't want to marry anyone now. I'll be happier on my own."

"You did say that," said Ivana. "But that was before you saw the duke's wealth. Think of how much of the land we passed through must be his. Amazing that it all belongs to one man." Ivana glowed at the thought of it.

"Land!" scoffed Talia. "I'm not interested in land. The more land you own, the more it ties you to it. Like a man, I suppose, who always wants you to stay in place while he goes where he will. Well, I don't want land, Ivana. I'd rather have my wealth in things that I can take with me."

Ivana looked as though she couldn't believe this. Someone who didn't think of land as the ultimate mark of wealth?

"As for your duke, it doesn't matter to me what he is hiding underneath that hood of his. He could be the most handsome man on the earth and I would still have no interest in him." Talia ended with an extravagant flourish and turned to move.

"Wait!" cried Ivana.

Talia turned back around, and the two of them stared at each other.

"Do you really think he is a bad choice for a marriage?" asked Ivana. She used her timid voice again, the one that had done whatever I bid her to do when first we found each other in the forest. I thought she had grown out of it since then.

Then again, I thought that Talia had grown out of her bullying, and it appeared that I was wrong on both scores. What had happened to the two loving sisters I had been so proud of bringing together? Their squabbling turned all my sacrifices vain.

Talia took a breath, and just when her face looked as though it would explode, she let it go. "He would be a terrible choice for me," she said at last, in almost as small a voice as Ivana.

"Oh." Ivana was disappointed. "Then perhaps I should—"

"'For me,' I said," Talia interrupted. "Not for you. I think he is very nearly perfect for you."

Ivana brightened. "Yes?"

"Yes," said Talia. "Except for the hood."

"Well," said Ivana soberly. "He is not the only one who is hiding his true face, then."

Talia seemed to have no quick reply to this and simply nodded her head. "I suppose."

There was a knock on the door.

"Yes?" said Talia and Ivana at the same time.

"Some refreshment from the duke," said a voice from behind the door.

"Come in, come in," said Talia.

Ivana moved forward to take the tray from the young man who held it. He limped on one good leg. The other was withered, and the hand on the same side as well. He was not an appealing sight, and I was reminded of the duke's first letter, when he spoke of his servants as family. The man must have a soft heart indeed to keep such a boy with him, despite all the clumsy mistakes he must make.

"I can do it, Miss," said the boy, and he maneuvered easily around Ivana, far more easily that I would have expected possible. He moved with all the grace and confidence of any boy his age. For that, I did not doubt, he could thank the duke and the duke alone.

Once the two glasses were poured, he handed them to Ivana and Talia, bowed, and went on his way, the tray tucked under one arm, and his withered leg dragging across the floor behind him.

Talia sniffed at her glass. "Ale? A bit strong before dinner, perhaps?" she asked critically. "Does he want to make sure that we are not in our full faculties tonight?"

One glass of ale? If he was trying to get them drunk, he'd best have sent a whole jug of the stuff.

But Ivana simply took a sip. "It is cider," she said and took another, larger swallow. "Very fine cider indeed."

"Hmmm," said Talia again, and took her own sip. She made a face. "Sour."

"I like it with an edge of sour," said Ivana.

I saw her look of confidence and thought how it mirrored the boy's. It seemed the duke had a capacity for bringing out the best in those around him. How different from my sister, who, from her own admission, had always kept at the castle the most stupid, most incompetent people in the world, so as to make herself look better in comparison.

Ivana sat gingerly on the side of the bed. She sank a little, but not so much she was in danger of drowning in the down.

"Well, perhaps there is nothing so terrible hidden under his hood, after all," said Talia, after a long sip at the cider. It was by way of an apology, I suppose.

"And perhaps I should not have said that you wished him back."

Talia laughed. "Let us make a pact," she said. "Between sisters, yes?"

"What is it?" asked Ivana.

Smart girl, I thought. If only I had thought to ask more questions before taking hold of my sister's mirror. How much heartache I might have saved myself. And I might even have been able to save her as well.

"No matter what happens to us, we will always be sisters. If you marry and have a dozen children—"

"A dozen?" whispered Ivana, then took a long draught of the cider.

"If I marry and move a thousand miles away, to live in some desert land where merchant women are valued and needed. If we never see each other again or if we see each other so often we are sick of it. It won't matter, for we are sisters."

"Yes," said Ivana. "Of course. We are sisters."

So, it was only a little spat. I needn't have worried their relationship was ever in any real jeopardy. But you see, I had never had a fight with my sister. I was coming to understand that such battles were not uncommon in other families, but in mine there was never any need for argument. My sister was too fine at manipulating me to do what she wanted anyway. And I was always too afraid of upsetting her, of turning her forever against me, to argue later.

So did that mean we did not love each other? No, I did not think it was fair to say that. We had loved each other, even at the end, even when we hated each other most. In a way, I suppose there had been an unspoken pact between us too. It was only her death that had cut us off at last.

"Mirror, you are wet," said Talia as she passed by me.

"The condensation from the room," I said irritably.

"It looks like tears," she said, with a hint of amusement in her voice. "Were you weeping for us, dear Mirror? Because you have never seen such true sisterly devotion as we have for each other?"

"Something like that," I said.

Talia took me into her room. "You see, it is every bit as big as Ivana's."

Although there were only two tapestries on the walls here. Besides that there was a painting of a small field with a hut in the background, and far in the distance a forest. I stared at the painting for a long while, making sure of every detail.

But this time I was convinced this was no coincidence. This was my sister's painting. How it had come to be here I could only guess. The duke might have purchased it and hung it here, but it was not a painting of great beauty. The strokes were too broad and the colors too dark for that. Also, there was a dust on the frame that led me to believe it was not the most honored piece in the room.

Was it original, then? Had this been the queen's palace

all those years before? And did this tell me anything of why she had not brought me here?

Another knock at the door and the same lame boy came to tell us the duke inquired if she was ready to dine.

"I am ready," said Talia. She had changed in the time I was thinking and now wore a muted gown of brown and gold. I had never seen her wear something so understated and yet so fitting. I wondered if it was a courtesy for Ivana, to let her shine.

And shine she did. As we came out of Talia's room, Ivana was coming out of hers. Though her features were hardly changed from the plain, sharp nose and swirling eyes I had first given her, she was stunning. It was the color in her cheeks, and the lift in her step.

We walked down the long staircase together, and I could not help but wonder how many times the queen had walked down these very steps. Had she ever once thought of me?

Chapter Twenty-Two

THE FIRE in the dining room licked hungrily at the logs. Behind us, we could hear the merchant's stomach growl loudly.

Talia turned and stared at him. "Father!" she scolded.

"Is it my fault the man sent only a glass of cider to fill my stomach?" asked Minitz. He patted himself, then belched. "It's been hours since I last ate, and you know how a journey weakens me." He spoke to Talia with no hesitation now, as his natural-born daughter who shared so many memories of the past with him.

"Where is the duke, anyway?" asked Minitz.

It was then that the duke appeared, still with the hood over his face. "Good evening, Merchant Minitz," he said, slightly inclining his head. He turned to Talia. "Miss Ivana." And once more, his gaze lingered on me.

Then last of all, to Ivana. "Miss Talia. I trust the cider I sent was suitable?"

"It was very good," said Talia.

"Yes, very fine," said Minitz, with a twist to his mouth.

The duke paid no attention to either of them. He had ears only for Ivana's words.

"I like cider with an edge of sour," said Ivana.

The duke's head went up and his shoulders straightened, as though he had suddenly grown two inches. If anyone could see inside his hood, I had no doubt his face would have beamed.

"Just so," he said. "I must show you my orchard. Tomorrow, perhaps. I have many apples there, but there is one tree in particular that is my favorite, for no other has apples as crisp or with the same sweet-sour flavor."

An apple tree with crisp apples and a sweet-sour flavor? I shook inside my glass. I had to see this tree. I could think of nothing I wanted less to do, and yet I could not avoid it. My sister was dead, but it seemed that the tree she had made of a witch was still alive. And so was I. Her magic had been terrible, but it had outlasted her.

The duke bent over the table to light the long, tapered red candles that were as dense as a forest. Servants moved around him silently and never once did they get in his way.

"Sit, sit," said the duke, making his way back to the head of the table. Merchant Minitz found his place next to the duke on the right hand. Ivana sat on his left, across from Merchant Minitz. Talia sat to her father's other side.

The duke clapped his hands, and a servant appeared with a tray of steaming mugs. "For our weary travelers."

Ivana sat me on the tabletop, then took her mug and lifted it to her lips. She sighed, then sipped again. From the satisfaction in her eyes, it was a good drink. For a moment I was jealous of her, that she could sigh and be satisfied by a mere drink. Then I told myself my time was over. It was enough that she have hers.

Minitz left his mug untouched in front of him. He stared at the duke's hood, but it was quite some time before the duke bothered to turn to him. Then, his host voice cold and proper, he said, "Is there something wrong?"

"It is only—" Minitz stumbled over the words. His hands pressed hard against the table. I thought perhaps he would give it up, whatever it was, in order to make the evening go more smoothly. But he did not.

"Yes, Merchant Minitz?" asked the duke.

"Your hood," he got out at last. "Is it not time to take it off? To show us all your true face? We are friends here, after all. We have given you no reason to be wary of us."

The duke hesitated. He had finished his steaming mug long ago, but he passed it back and forth, left to right. Finally, he set it aside and turned his hood to

Minitz. "If you have given me no reason to be wary, others have. I mean no disrespect, but I will reveal myself in good time, in the place and manner which I choose." He stretched out his hands and used a consoling tone. "Now, shall we enjoy our dinner?"

I looked over the long table. Silver glinted everywhere. Clearly the duke had spared nothing for this occasion but the revelation of the face hidden under his hood.

Servants came again to take the mugs, now drained, and other servants brought in fine, fresh bread from the kitchen. Ivana and Minitz both ate heartily, but Talia only picked at her piece. She stared at the duke's hooded face and shivered.

"Are you cold?" asked the duke solicitously. "Shall I have the fire stoked for you?"

"No, no," she muttered.

But the duke motioned to a servant nonetheless, and the fire was soon raging. Then came the great platters of the main course. Roast duck with wild berry sauce, and soups, hot and cold. Pickled hog's feet. Sausages. Cheeses.

The duke ate sparingly under his hood, and it was not long before Ivana was conscious of this. She looked at Talia, still staring at the duke, and I saw her try to catch Talia's eye to warn her to stop, but in vain. Neither of them could see any hint of the duke's true face, but as a platter was set before the duke, I had a glimpse reflecting into the silver, and for the first time, I began to doubt that Ivana would be happy with this man.

Yes, she had said she did not care what he looked like. Yes, I knew that she had few expectations of marriage other than kindness and a few comforts. But this face—no wonder the man wore a hood! Who could live with a face like that staring back day after day? If I knew Ivana at all, I would guess she would try. But how could it not wear on her? And then what would the duke feel for her?

Yet what could I do? I was again in a position of not being able to speak what I knew. But if I could, there was still no warning for this.

When the dishes were cleared away at last, and real ale was served, Merchant Minitz stood and offered a toast. "To my daughter's marriage. May it be as happy as mine, and much longer."

But before he could take a sip, the duke held up a hand. "Wait," he said in a voice that even the merchant had to obey. The queen had commanded others a thousand times while I heard her, and yet her voice had never been obeyed without fear. The duke's was.

The duke fingered his hood. Had he found courage in the faces set before him, or hope? I did not think he had intended to do this so soon.

"You don't have to," Ivana whispered.

"Do you not wish it?" asked the duke, turning to her quickly.

"No, that's not what I meant. If you wish to show me your face, show me. But let it be your choice. As you said." There was something in her voice that made me think she had guessed already. Perhaps sometime in the course of the dinner she too had seen a glimpse in the flashing silver of a tray or the distorted image of a glass.

"No. I will not be a coward before you of all people. If we are to be married, there must be honesty between us from the beginning. Only then can trust grow, as I hope it will." The duke brought himself to his full height, and in one swift movement, as if he had practiced this for weeks in anticipation, he put back his hood.

It was an unforgettable sight.

Talia put a hand to her mouth and gasped.

Merchant Minitz drew back in horror. He put a hand to Ivana's shoulder, as if to protect her from looking on such a thing.

But Ivana had already seen. She froze, but more with pity than anything else, I thought.

Dark eyes smoldered out of a ruined face: eyebrows burned away, nose pushed in, a twisted mouth, deep scars that ran across each cheek. If not for the way in which the duke stood, with dignity and even a challenge to his eyes, I would have felt sorry for him. But there could be no pity offered to this man.

"You will think I have deceived you." The duke nodded to Merchant Minitz, but I think his words were more for Ivana than for anyone else. "I must apologize for that, and beg your forgiveness, if you think you have any left to offer me." His voice was quiet, as deep as before, though perhaps more persuasive.

"But—why?" asked Merchant Minitz.

The duke barked out a laugh. "Look into your daughter's face. Look into your own face, for that matter." The duke waved a hand at me, the mirror. "There needs to be no more answer than that."

No one spoke.

Perhaps the silence would have gone on forever, but the duke broke it himself. "I told you before I had reason to be wary. You do not know how many times this scene has played itself out before. How many young ladies I have invited to my home, shown myself to, and then watched recoil in cold horror. I had learned not to hope—until I met you and heard you speak of your daughter's forthrightness, yet innate goodness. I knew that I could trust her to tell me the truth immediately, without any mincing. I thought that with all that, it might have been possible—" A bleak smile crossed his face. "Ha! I was a fool again."

He covered his head once more, then turned to leave. "You need not say anything, Miss Talia. I know already what you are thinking. Your whole body speaks for you."

"And what does it say?" asked Ivana, her hands pushing palm-down at the table, her voice like fire.

The duke turned to her, moving stiffly. "What?"

"Iv—Talia," Merchant Minitz stuttered over the name, then shook his head and gave it up. She knew who she was. "I am sorry. I thought this was a good match. But of course I did not know this—" A short gesture. Even Merchant Minitz could not bear to see that face in full. "What father would wish his daughter to marry a man like this?" he asked.

Ivana acted as though Merchant Minitz had never spoken. She stared into the duke's eyes. "What does my body say? When it speaks so obviously to you?"

He held up his hands in a helpless gesture. "That I am repellant to you."

"Well, I hope that I have read your letters better than you have read me."

"My letters?" One hand twitched until he put it down, pinned by the other.

"Or were they lies? Did you make up the man the letters showed inside of you? Was he not real, after all?"

"Real? Of course the letters are real. But—" He gestured to the hood.

"You think what is under your hood matters to me? When a face can change in a single day? An accident—or a bit of magic? It is what is past the face that I must see. I thought your letters showed me a portion of that. I hoped that coming here would show me more. But if all you have to display is your face, then . . ."

This was the unflinching Ivana I had seen only twice before, when she had gone to save Talia from Blenin, and when she had confronted the witch in the marketplace.

"Wait," whispered the duke. He put his hand out to Ivana, and she touched it. "Tell me what I must say to you to gain another chance."

"I need no magic words," said Ivana.

The duke said nothing in response, but there was a change in his bearing. His back drew straighter, and his head, still hooded, rose another foot in height. Then he clapped his hands once more.

Three servants arrived to do his bidding.

"Take them to their rooms," he commanded.

Merchant Minitz and Talia both moved eagerly away from the duke. But Ivana lingered, holding me in her hands.

"We will speak again in the morning," said the duke softly. It was a promise, and a plea.

"Yes," said Ivana.

As she followed the servants up the steps, I realized that for the space of an evening, I had almost forgotten that I was a mirror. I had felt alive again. Perhaps this was as close to being human as I would ever be. If so, I would be content.

Chapter Twenty-Three

IN THE MORNING, the duke took Ivana out to view his garden and zoo. She did not take me with her, so I had to interpret her reactions when she returned and described the experience.

"The animals are so tame," she said, her eyes aglow. "There was a lion that leaped to the duke when we came in sight. I was terrified that it would attack him, but the duke put his hand up and let the lion lick at it."

"Ugh," said Talia.

"No. Its tongue was long and pink and soft." She blushed. "It was like a kiss."

Like a kiss? And when had she learned what a kiss felt like?

"Oh?"

Ivana nodded vigorously. "The duke is not truly ugly, you know," she said.

Talia made a small face.

"Of course, there are the scars. But his hands are warm and strong. And his hair is so rich and thick, with a hint of curl in it just above his ears."

I did not remember his ears. It must mean that they hadn't been ruined like the rest.

Ivana sighed. "I can almost imagine what he might have looked like, if he had not been damaged so."

Well, it seemed her imagination was better than mine or Talia's, but it was just as well. I had not anticipated that Ivana would find a marriage that was more than mutual kindness. In time, perhaps there might be passion as well, all the passion that I had never had a chance to experience for myself.

"What else?" asked Talia.

"Well, he showed me his apple trees. He has sixty different kinds, from black to gold to red and green."

I felt suddenly very fragile. Apple trees here in this place could only remind me of one thing. "Did he show you the tree that made the cider of last night?" I asked, ready to shatter at a breath.

"Yes," said Ivana.

"Crimson apples with a touch of white on them?" I asked.

"Yes," she said again. "Why do you ask?"

I had to think of a reason I could give to her. I did not

want to tell her about the queen, about what I had been. What would Ivana think of me if she had known I had aided in such terrible things? I knew that there was little she could do for me now, but still I valued her good opinion of me. What else did I have?

"I remember tasting an apple that color once," I said. Letting my voice go hoarse with longing was not at all difficult. "It was the last fruit I ever ate, and it was so delicious I thought I would never need to eat again. If only I could remember that taste forever . . ."

"Oh," said Ivana. "I am so sorry. I did not realize—"

I had not meant to make her feel a vampire in sucking out this old memory. Well, at least it would keep her far from the truth.

"Where was the tree?" I asked.

Ivana closed her eyes. "In the far corner. By the end of the garden wall."

"Are you sure?" I asked.

She looked at me quizzically.

I should not have asked the location. There was no reason for me to care about that. "Perhaps you were too far away from it to see clearly," I said.

Ivana shook her head. "No, we walked everywhere. The duke said that I should see all the trees, every one. They are to be mine too, and he said I should love them each as he did."

"'The duke said—'" Talia echoed, teasing. "It sounds as though you find him every inch the man you had thought from the letters."

But Ivana was all seriousness. "More," she said fiercely. "Much more." And blushed again.

"Have you thought of letting me use my magic to change his face?" I asked, after a moment's thought. The duke's face would be easier to change than Talia's or Ivana's had been. I would only be restoring what was already there, not changing the bones or the shape of the features. Then Ivana would not need her imagination to make him as handsome as he should have been, in her eyes or in anyone else's.

Yes, it might cost me my voice, my last link with humanity. But I wanted so much for Ivana's happiness to be complete. It might well be the last thing I could do for her.

"I thought you needed the magic for yourself," said Ivana. "To be human again."

"Oh, I shall find more easily enough," I lied. "But think of the duke!"

Ivana thought.

Too long, for Talia tired of the silence. "Ivana, you must ask him if he will allow it," she said. "Think how much easier his life would be—and yours—if he could show himself freely, never worrying what the reaction would be. I wonder that he has never thought of it before."

Yes. A man as wealthy and powerful as Duke Fensky had surely had opportunities before to change himself. Yet he had never used them. Why? There had to be a reason.

"I do not want him to think that I want it," said Ivana. "I said last night that it was not his face that mattered."

"Of course it isn't to you. But to others," said Talia. "Think how closed off he has been here in his castle all these years."

Ivana thought this over. "All right. I will ask him," she said. "I will try to find a time before we leave."

Merchant Minitz knocked on the door as the girls prepared for dinner. "We could leave," he said abruptly. "He will not force us to stay here if we do not wish to, though he has already done much to prepare for the wedding."

"I think it is up to Ivana," said Talia.

Minitz turned to Ivana. "So, Ivana. Do we stay or go?"

Ivana smiled firmly. "I will stay," she said.

Minitz nodded. "And shall we tell him the truth? That you are Ivana and she is Talia?"

Ivana went white around the lips. "No. Not now."

Minitz put a hand out to Ivana to steady her. "I did not mean to disturb you. You must believe me, I did not. But—why not tell him your secret? He has told you his. And if you are truly to be married, you should share with him your true name. He cannot possibly think the matter of a name more important than that of a face."

Ivana shook her head, adamant.

"If you are sure?" asked Merchant Minitz.

"I am sure," said Ivana. "I will tell him. Later."

Did she mean after the wedding? I watched her and decided not. She might not leave much time before, but she was too honest to marry in bad faith. And she was brave enough when she had to be as well. I would not forget that about her, no matter what happened to me.

"Hopefully I will not make a mistake at dinner then." With that, the merchant let the girls get back to dressing. This time, it was Talia who told Ivana what to wear, for Ivana would not have cared if she had on tar and feathers. Or nothing at all.

Once we began down the stairs, I felt Ivana's hand dig into my glass. It reminded me of the queen, and of the witch at the market. But Ivana had never been interested in possessing me. She would feel a pang at losing me, but she would let me go if I told her I wished it.

But I did not wallow in my gloomy thoughts, for the second dinner was as magnificent as the first. The room was dressed as before, and with a clap of the duke's hands, a barrage of pies, meats, and drinks began. The final course was a frozen dish made of cream and sugar. I enjoyed Ivana's delight as she took her first bite.

"You like it?" asked the duke. He had his hood on, as before.

"It is wonderful," said Ivana. She took another bite to prove it.

Talia and Merchant Minitz watched her, and took courage to try their own bowls.

"It is an old recipe. My mother's mother's."

The fire would have melted the cream, but it was eaten too quickly. When the dishes had been scraped clean, the duke stood and invited us all to follow him to his drawing room.

There he served peppermint tea with his own hands, so as to ensure privacy. There was a moment of silence, and I suppose Talia thought it a good time to broach the question of my magic.

"Talia has a question to ask you, don't you, Talia?" she said.

The duke seemed distracted a moment, then nodded courteously. "Talia, of course."

Ivana held me out. "This—my mirror—it has—it might—"

Well, her happiness with the duke certainly did not help her speaking abilities.

"What is it you wish to say?" The duke's voice was gentle, and he tugged his hood back an inch from his head, so that we had no choice but to see his smashed nose and twisted mouth once more. "You know there is no reason to be afraid of me."

"Magic," Ivana got out at last. "The mirror is magic."

"Yes?" His voice was like rumbling stone. I could not tell what it meant.

"It can change—faces. I wondered if you wanted it to change yours."

It was not the most delicate way to put such a thing. But the duke's reaction did not seem to be bad. He was silent a moment. Then he pulled his hood as far over his head as he could. When he spoke again, it was with a perfectly normal voice. Too normal, I thought.

"You do not know, perhaps, that I was third-born son," he began. "My two brothers both died shortly after birth. My mother blamed the physician who attended her. She said he was not clean. So when she felt me quickening, she did not tell my father or ask for aid. Instead, she secretly brought a village midwife to the castle." The duke waved a hand behind him, to the village we had passed on our way, the village so close to the one from which Ivana herself had come.

"At first, my mother said that she was very pleased with the midwife because she felt better after each meeting. It was as if the midwife, by merely touching her belly, was able to make the child inside it healthier. My mother became sure that I would not die at birth, as had my brothers. She was so sure that she told my father the truth about the midwife who had been coming to see her."

The duke took a long breath, but I could not see more than his hands, which were straight at his sides as he spoke, as though the tale were about some other man. "As soon as my father heard the midwife's name, he was furious. The woman was a witch, a known worker in the dark art. She had already stolen from others to extend her overlong life. And his wife—his heir—was under her care?"

I had never known of a witch who could steal life so slowly that it was not entirely taken away. It was a good trick for a witch, but I found I had no interest in discovering it for myself. I had been a witch, once. I had thought I would go back to it. But thinking of what had become of the duke, of the queen who had taken wherever she could and the witch at the market, storing deaths until they were of use to her—it was unbearable. How could I take magic to be human again, if this was the cost? What right did I have to steal life from another?

"So it is magic that stole your face. Not some accident," said Merchant Minitz. "Or nature."

The duke nodded.

"But how did she do it?" asked Talia. "After your father told her she could not come back? She was angry then, and wished for revenge?"

The duke shook his head. "No. The witch had already

taken from me. All along, she had been taking from me. The feeling of wholeness she gave to my mother was false, entirely false."

A long silence followed. Even the fire seemed to stop crackling, in respect of the duke's naked history.

"I have always thought of magic," said the duke after a while, "as the opposite of love. Love gives. Magic takes. Where love is, there is no need for magic. And where magic is, there can be no love."

Yes, I thought. He had it. It had been the magic that destroyed me and my sister, and it had nearly destroyed Talia and Ivana as well. If the duke took it to himself, it could destroy the new and fragile love that had stretched between him and Ivana.

The duke stood and poked the fire back to crackling. Then he turned to the group before him. "It is late. We should go to bed now. In the morning, we can speak again, of happier things."

Chapter Twenty-Four

AS IVANA TOOK me to her room, I thought more on the love my sister and I had once shared. In my bitterness, I had pushed the good memories away and held tight to the bad. But in the early days, there had been many demonstrations of love, in my sister's own way. One of the best was the day my sister found a kitten floating in the stream.

The little creature must have found its way out of a sack, thrown there by some peasant who had too many mouths to feed already. But my sister fetched it out of the stream, either by magic or by her own hand, and brought the tiny bundle to me.

"Here," she said gruffly.

"What is it?" I asked, thinking it was already dead, and she expected me to make dinner from its flesh and soup from its bones. But then it sneezed, and I put out my arms. I cradled the unexpected gift, marveling at the delicate fur and the splintered color of the eyes.

"You could have taken its life," I said. I thought she took everything for her magic.

She shrugged. "It would not have had much magic in it," she said. "A creature that small, only barely living."

I held the creature tightly, feeling its tiny heart beating next to mine. Its life had so nearly slipped away into the water. But my sister had saved it, for me. Once in her life, she had chosen love over magic.

"Mirror?" asked Ivana as she put me down next to the elaborately carved headboard. There were creatures of the forest peering out from every nook and cranny in it: deer, rabbits, squirrels, mice, even a small black bear.

"Yes?"

"I think the duke does not want magic to change him."

Well, that was obvious!

But she continued, hesitantly. "I think he may not wish for me to have a magic mirror at all."

Ah, so here it came at last. I had thought I was prepared for it, but I could not deny the sting I felt at her rejection.

"I will have to tell him who I am," said Ivana. "I meant to all along, but now I wonder if he will marry me once he knows the truth. If so, then I will not have to worry about you. We will go home together."

"You mean you think he will send you away because of the magic?" I asked.

She bowed her head.

"But you were magicked nearly as unwillingly as he was," I said. "And he cannot expect you to use magic to take back your old face when he will not use magic to take back his." If he was logical, that is.

"I hope so," said Ivana. "But then what of you, Mirror? Shall I send you back to Minitz's house, with Talia? Would you mind that?" She said it as if the words were choking her.

"No." I pretended nonchalance. "I do not mind at all." Though secretly I could only think of ways in which I could convince Talia to throw me in front of the horses. That seemed far less painful than living on without hope.

"I will make Talia promise to get you the magic you need," Ivana went on. "And if the duke gives me any money, I will send it to you without telling him what it is for."

"I do not think that lies are a good beginning to a marriage," I told her, though what did I know of that kind of love? I had never had a chance to fall in love with a man, good or evil. There had only ever been my sister for me.

Ivana hung her head. "Perhaps not," she said. "But

surely there is something I can do for you. After all you have done for me."

There was a terrible irony in this. All I had done for her? It had all been done selfishly. Yet it had turned out well, hadn't it? How had that happened? In a hundred years, perhaps my capacity for love had grown while I had remained stagnant in every other way.

"Be happy with him. That is all I ask of you," I said.

"Oh, I will," said Ivana.

"And besides," I said, "I think I may be better off with Talia anyway. I have the feeling she will be a very good merchant woman, in not too long. And even if I never find the magic to become myself again, I will be able to see the world at her side."

"Yes," said Ivana, but it was clear she had seen enough of the world to last her a whole lifetime. She only wanted a place to settle now, and a man to settle with. Who better than the duke, who would leave his home but rarely?

"If you are with Talia," said Ivana, "I hope that you would not mind if I came to visit you now and then. I think the duke will allow me that, don't you?"

"No reason he shouldn't." If my voice was stiff, it was because I was afraid of losing my composure. That would not help Ivana at all.

"And if you do—go back to what you were—you

could come visit me as well. I would be very glad to see you, Mirror."

"Mira," I said. "My name is Mira."

"Mira," said Ivana.

There was a silence then, but it was a wonderful one. In calling me by my name, Ivana had restored part of my humanity already, without any magic at all. It had only taken her love.

Suddenly the door opened without a knock and Talia slipped in. She wore a thick robe over her nightclothes, and shivered even so.

"Are you not freezing in here?" she asked, holding her arms around some hidden object in her robe. By the shape, I guessed it was a book of some kind.

Ivana stared at the small fire that had been left in the grate and stepped away from it, looking out the window. "I was always cold at home," she said. She gestured toward the window.

"I do not know how you survived it," said Talia, moving closer to the fire.

"I survived worse than the cold," said Ivana.

Talia looked stricken at the reminder. "I did not mean to open old wounds," she said.

Ivana shook her head and smiled faintly. "Not wounds anymore." She pointed at the lump in Talia's robe. "So, what do you have there?" she asked. "Something of the duke's?"

"I doubt it." She pulled out a book but kept the front cover hidden. I felt a strange patch of blackness across my glass as I stared at it. "I found it in a hidden drawer in my dresser. If the duke knew it was there, he would surely have burned it long ago."

"Burned it? Is it magic, then?"

Talia smiled and opened the book. "Listen to this," she said.

A SPELL FOR LOVE

CALL A NAME, THE ONE YOU WISH.
BREAK HIS HEART WITH A DISH.
YOU WILL PIECE THE BITS TOGETHER.
GLUE THEM IN THE DARKEST WEATHER.

Talia would have gone on except that Ivana snatched the book away. "Don't mock him like that!" she cried.

"It wasn't mockery," Talia insisted, moving around Ivana to try to get the book back. "I thought it might help."

"I don't need the help of a magic book," said Ivana. "I have his love already."

Talia stopped fighting and turned to the fire. "Do you?" she said. "Are you certain it's not just relief on his part that someone finally can bear the sight of his face?"

Ivana turned pale with spots of color on each cheek. "It is not just relief," she said. But there was fear in her voice.

"Magic would make sure of it," said Talia.

"No. I won't do it. He would never forgive it."

I was glad that Ivana knew that much about her duke, at least. It boded well for her future with him.

"Well, there are other spells. Perhaps one for me." Talia held out her hand.

Ivana did not give the book away so easily. "If you found it here, then it must have been hidden by some evil witch." Her eyes grew bright. "Perhaps the witch who stole the duke's face from him as a babe. Do you really wish to trust yourself to the magic of that witch?" she asked.

She took a step closer to the fire. I wondered if she would throw the book in. I half hoped that she would. I was beginning to guess what the cover of the book would say, but if I had no chance to see it, then there would be no dilemma for me. I had enough dilemmas for a hundred lives, I thought.

"If it did come from an evil witch, that does not mean the magic itself is evil," argued Talia. "Why not use the spells for good?"

Ivana shook her head, biting her lower lip.

"Let's ask the mirror," said Talia. "Mirror, what do

you think?" She motioned to the book, and Ivana reluctantly held up its cover. I saw *Transformations and Transmutations* written in that old, familiar spidery hand. Black ink on blood red leather. And the smell of well used magic, ancient as days.

It couldn't be. But it was.

I ached to turn the pages, to see if the spells inside were what they had been when Zerba and I looked together. But I had no arms, no hands, no fingers. It was infuriating, impossible! I had never thought of this book in all my plans to regain myself. I had thought it was lost forever, but it must have been here all along. My sister had taken it here. And she had left me in the hideaway.

Why? The answer seemed obvious. Because inside those two covers was a spell that would allow me my independence again, and she could not have that. I had to be bound to her forever, and longer.

"How about this one?" asked Talia. Could it have been entirely innocent that she turned to the page on transforming mirrors? But she did not even look at the words herself as she held it up to me.

I thought about all the reasons I had given myself for giving up my quest. The duke's argument against magic. To keep Ivana and Talia safe. To prove I had changed.

But the words were right in front of me. I had only to speak them aloud, and the spell itself would draw the magic from all around. I had told myself I would not use magic, but what would it hurt? If the witch whose magic was close by was stolen from, should I try to prevent that for her sake?

"Or this one?" asked Talia, turning to another page.

But this one had a spell for transforming a tree. It seemed more complicated than the spell for a mirror, but perhaps that is because a tree can learn to be happy as it is, to stretch roots for water, to make leaves and branches each year, to rest through winter. But a mirror can never be happy. A mirror must always remember what it was, and wish to return.

"Or this?" asked Talia, turning yet again.

This time the spell was for turning a peasant girl into a duchess, not just in body but in heart.

"Well?" asked Talia, craning her head down so that she could try to read the words upside down.

"That one's useless," I said without even reading it. For if my sister had had this book, she would have used it on herself. And it had never worked. She had never overcome her past, not even when she was the wealthiest, most powerful queen in the world. At heart, she had always been the starving peasant girl whose family had sent her away, the witch's apprentice who was abused by the village children.

And for all the love I claimed to have felt for her, I had

never worked the true transformation. Strange that I had never thought of it this way before. All those times she had given me magic, poured it into me, hoping I would pour it back to her—had she wanted me to do more than change her face?

"Are they all useless then?" asked Talia. "Not a real book of spells, after all?" Her disappointment was nothing like mine. "I thought it looked so old, it must be real. Maybe the duke knew about it after all and only kept it as a relic of the past. Something to remind him that not all magic has power."

Ivana sighed. "Yes, that must be it," she said. The book had lost all importance for her as well.

Talia set the book down at her bedside and put me next to it. It was my own fault that I would have to be tortured this way, yet I dared not tell her the truth. The fire flared with a burst of wind, then nearly died out as the two girls slipped under the bedcovers and found their ease with each other once more.

"I think you and the duke would not have suited each other," said Ivana sleepily.

Talia giggled. "I suppose at best we might have learned to feel compassion for each other."

I listened with only half my attention.

"My parents never did," said Ivana. "You see, my father stole my mother from a nearby village when she was very young, younger than either of us. My father often said that she was entirely useless to him, always complaining, never helping with the work unless he beat her to it. He had never learned how to love."

I felt a stinging, as though a bee had somehow broken through my glass. Ivana's words were nearly exactly the same ones that Zerba had once used to describe my sister. Though I had long hidden the memory even from myself, it came back to me in a flash. The night had been dark and eerie—filled with my sister's cries of frustration. She had failed in something magical and could not be comforted.

"I wish I could help her," I said.

"You don't have the magic to help her," said Zerba. She licked at her fingers and put out the little light that had brought warmth to her hut. Then she added matter-of-factly, "You must know you will never be the witch that she is."

Zerba had always tended to the blunt, but I was crushed. Zerba waved a hand at my hurt. "Do not misunderstand me, child. I meant only that there is more to your life than magic," she added. "But magic is all for her."

I told myself that Zerba was wrong, that I mattered to my sister. But what if she was right, and it had been my place to supply what my sister had been missing? All these years I thought I had been looking for my freedom. And the queen had looked so long for more beauty, more power. What if we had both been blind to what we truly needed?

Ivana settled herself in her bed, and Talia whispered good night. The two fell asleep wrapped in each other's arms, perhaps for the last time. As for me, I lay next to the book of spells through the night, stirring up good memories of my sister.

I remembered the day Zerba had died. I knew her magic had not been taken from her, for her body was still warm with it as it lay near the mound of dirt that would be her grave. I wandered, weeping, back to the hut that had been hers. All around it there were tiny flowers the color of blood, poking up from under the snow. Like Zerba, the flowers were small and insignificant. I knew that my sister had made them. She had used her magic for something that did not enhance either her beauty or her power.

Later, she had been different. Perhaps it was because she had given up hope in me. And so she had gone on, building her magic, destroying love everywhere she found it. For why should others have love if she could not?

I found that I hardly blamed her, when I thought about it this way. I could not even be afraid of her anymore. I could only feel sorry for her, and wish I could speak to her one last time. But of course that was impossible.

Chapter Twenty-Five

AS THE WIND howled outside, I could smell the magic of the witch from the marketplace grow stronger. The spell book next to me would use her magic first of all, it being the most available. And why not? Her magic basket was filled with those living in death. If I took from them, it would be a mercy. To use up their magic would set them free. Not to do so when given the chance would be cruel.

And then there was my sister's rival, now the duke's crimson and white apple tree. I knew how to transform her now as well. I had both spells memorized. If I made a promise to myself not to become a witch again, not to use magic for my own again, then surely it was right for me to undo what I had ruined.

Quickly, before reason returned to me, I spoke the spell that I had waited so long to use:

Mirror, mirror, on the wall
Stretch your hands straight and tall.
Feel your toes against the floor.
You will break the magic door.

Mirror, mirror, on the wall
Break the glass and break the thrall.
Your own face comes back to you
And all that's human through and through.

I said the words once and felt a tingling sensation at the base of my wood. I said them again and felt a humming reverberating through my glass. A third time and there was a crack. I pushed myself into that crack, straining at the magic around me. I could taste the air in my lungs. I could feel the cool of the fall morning. I could smell the embers of the fire mingled with apples from the orchard beyond.

All this time I had hoped for this, but I do not think I had ever believed it would come to pass. I could feel a finger, the left index finger, poke through the glass. Then a rush of exhilaration as I prepared myself for the final shattering of glass, not in death this time, but in life.

I tried to push through the glass harder. It had felt so fluid before. Now it would not budge. It was as strong as any stone. I wiggled my finger in desperation, but it melted into mist and then it was gone. Soon the crack in the glass through which I had drawn that other magic drew the magic back, and more.

I chanted the spell again, but I could hardly hear myself speak. The spell had taken my magic first. And what of the witch from the marketplace whom I had thought it would take from as well? I should have known she would fight against it, that she would have some defense against this spell book. Now I was blind and deaf and mute. I could not even warn Ivana and Talia to throw me out the window so that the witch whose magic the spell had tried to take would come only for me.

As I lay there, defenseless, I wondered how the witch could have known this specific book of spells. She would have had to study the book intensely to protect herself in this way. The spells were ruthless in their quest for magic to use to activate themselves. They had been made that way when first written down. Perhaps this witch was also the one from the duke's past. Perhaps she had had a chance to see this book on her many visits to the duke's pregnant mother.

It made a certain kind of sense, but there was another possibility that echoed in my head. What if she had not found the book but left it here? What if the reason her magic seemed familiar to me was because it was part of me?

I hoped that the girls would wake in the morning and

try to rouse me. When they could not, they might take me to the duke. If he heard the whole truth at last, I felt sure he would destroy me, and that was far better than what I feared would happen if the witch came for me.

But gradually light dawned on my face, and I could taste the magic that flowed around me, the old, tortured flavor of it. It was doubly familiar now, with its long-dying breaths, screams for release, betrayals, and dying despairs. How could I have failed to recognize it before? Because I had not wanted to know how horrible she had become?

I did not fight the magic coming into me. It would have made no difference anyway. But she did not give me much, only enough to have my vision again, and my voice, though I did not use it. I stared out into the expanse of trees, apple trees, and saw the bulk of the castle beyond a stone wall. I was no longer in Ivana's room, but outside in the cold morning of a new fall day. I could have wept at the thought that I had been so close to feeling the chill of it on my face, my fingertips, my shoulders. But I was only a mirror. Still, as ever.

"So, little Mirror," said a voice. "I have found you again."

She held me up to her, and I could see the face of my sister, the queen, staring back at me. Her eye was still wounded from the rock Talia had thrown in the marketplace, but there was no mistaking her. I did not know why she treated me as a stranger, but it hardly mattered now.

"You are more than you first seemed when we met at the market, aren't you?" she asked.

If I was, then so was she. The witch from the market. My sister, the queen. And the witch who had taken the duke's brothers, and his face as well. I had been so concerned with Ivana and Talia, and with myself, that I had not tested her magic deeply enough. I had not felt the old neediness and the cruelty. Perhaps I had not been ready to know her true identity until now.

"A mirror like you is quite a find," she went on cheerfully. "I could have spent much of my magic making such a thing, and then where would I have found the woman to place inside? So few women would have survived such a transformation, you know. And more would have let themselves die in a year or two. What reason does a mirror have to live, after all?"

A good question. I was not sure my answer was as good. "I always thought I would be human again," I said softly, playing along with her strange game—if game it was.

She laughed heartily at that. "And why would you think that?" she asked.

No more game. Now was the time to be direct, to set things back as they were, and first and foremost, our relationship. We had been sisters, after all. "You," I said.

There was a slight shift in her gaze, but she shook it off, refusing to understand me. "You mean, you thought you could steal the magic from me?" she said. "But what kept you hoping before that, little Mirror? You are past the time of despair, for I can tell from the strength of the bond that you have been wood and glass for many decades now."

"What kept me hoping?" I echoed. "You mean 'who' kept me hoping."

She waved a hand. It was clearly a crone's hand. And her back was still hunched over with years.

I had changed her face, but I had not changed any more than that.

"Who, then?" she asked, her face intent and very large in my glass. "Was it another witch somewhere? With power like mine? If you want revenge on her, I can assure you, there is no better chance than now."

"No other witch," I said, impatient now with her denial of the past. What was the point of it now that I was here before her? "It was you. It was always you."

But there was genuine confusion in her face, and distress as well. She was afraid she had a weakness. Perhaps I was her weakness. "What are you saying? I never saw you before that day in the market."

"Oh no?" Was this part of the reason I had not recognized her? Because she did not recognize herself? Well, she would when I was done with her. "What happened to you a hundred years ago?" I demanded. "Do you remember nothing of your life then? Of the king and the castle and the beautiful princess you went out to kill with a poisoned apple from this tree?"

"Princess? King? Apple? I don't know what you are talking about. Are you mad? Or are you trying to distract me to save yourself?" She pulled her magic closer then and stepped away from me. But I knew she was remembering, even if she did not want to.

Yet why would she not want to? That was the real question. Perhaps there was something different in her, the beginnings of a deep change that needed only to be finished.

"Not to save me," I said. "To save you." For now I knew that if I had wished escape from my prison, I could have let the warrior bash me in with his axe, or coaxed the old fortune-teller to break me accidentally. But Ivana and Talia had taught me that sisters had an obligation to each other. And my sister needed me. She was drowning in her evil, and she could not save herself. Only I could, if I could make her my sister once again.

"Save me? Ha! What a story that is. Little Mirror, whatever witch made you did not teach you your proper place, I can tell. Perhaps she let you think of yourself as more than a servant, but to me you are nothing more than that."

"Oh no?" I asked. "Are you sure of that?"

Her words were certain, but her manner was not. Her arms were folded over her sagging stomach, and her eyes were wary, darting here and there. She was afraid of me, a little mirror, as she said, with no more magic than it took to speak. But ah, what I could say!

"Tell me, where were you born? Who were your parents? What do you remember of your early days?" I insisted, prodding and poking at whatever scabs had healed over her memories.

"I don't have to answer that," she said. She turned her head to the side, as if that would keep me from speaking.

And yet, she did not silence me. She could so easily have done it, as she had before. Just strip me of my last bit of magic, make me a slave rather than a servant. But she did not do it. She could not, not to me.

"Where did you learn your magic? When did you first find that old book of spells that I tried to use against you?"

"It was here," she insisted. "Here all along. I found it quite by chance, one day when I was visiting the duchess."

"Oh? And though it was written by a powerful and wily wizard a thousand years ago, you were still able to protect yourself from it in a few cursory glances? You were able to use its spells without anyone to teach you to unlock it?" This was a guess, but by her startled reaction, a correct one.

Now I dug deeper into the cold ashes of the past, hoping they would stir to fire. "Your life more than a hundred years ago—tell me of it."

"A hundred years?" She stopped all movement, and her eyes grew small and focused. "What do you know about what happened to me a hundred years ago?"

I told her all that I knew. The queen had gone after the princess and her prince. She had set her magic against their love. But her magic must have lost. Perhaps that was what had devastated her memory, though it had not killed her.

"Tell me what you remember," I said softly. As a sister might, pleading gently.

"I remember waking at the bottom of a great ravine," she said hesitantly, as though this was the first time she had allowed herself to think of it. "I was drained of magic, so much that it was two days before I gathered enough to heal the broken legs that had caught my fall." She rubbed at one thigh absently, ironing out an old ache.

"I can take away that pain for you," I offered.

"You can?" She was suspicious.

"Just give me the magic to do it," I said. "I will change your whole body, back to what it was all that time ago, to the beautiful queen I remember." And I trembled at the risk I took.

"Ha! You will steal the magic from me, and keep it for yourself," she suggested. "It is a trick."

"I swear to you, it is no trick."

"But you've wanted to be human again all this time. It's what you've lived for." I thought that perhaps she did remember a little of the past, but none of the best of it, only that I had hated her and that magic had always been between us.

"Trust me," I said.

"Trust you? I've never trusted anyone in my life." But she did not laugh this time. I could feel her hands on my wood, sticky with cold sweat.

"I know," I said. "But trust me now."

She considered it for a moment, and then another. "I will only give you enough to transform me a bit at a time," she said. "Then I will make sure that you cannot use it for yourself, and that you do it properly."

"No," I said.

She lifted a hand and brought down a long, pointed fingernail. It scratched into my glass, and I felt parts of my vision go dark and numb. This was a magical attack, and there would never be a cure for it. Even if I were human, I would not be able to see or hear clearly in those places ever again.

"Do it!" she demanded.

"No," I said a second time. Doubt assailed me.

"You will do as I say!" She pushed her magic into me once more, this time filling me with the roaring sound of weeping and wailing. The voices were so close that I would never forget them, not if I lived another hundred years. Their pain would be mine forever.

"No." I said it again, and I could see her utter frustration. Her teeth were tearing at her long fingernails. Her feet were stomping on the ground. Her mouth was shouting soundlessly.

But she could not make me do it. A realization at last. Calm followed. If I was wrong about her, about the heart that lay deep inside all her magic, then I would gladly die for it. And if I was not wrong, then I could not fail her.

"You must trust me." A last and final plea.

"I will not trust anyone," she said. "Do you think I have survived all these years—many more than a hundred if anything you say is right—do you think it is because I have made myself vulnerable to those who could betray me?"

"I will not betray you," I said. And to myself I wondered if it might have been better if she had not lived all these hundred years. Sometimes another day of life is not worth the cost. Sometimes death is to be preferred, if it is a happy death.

But magic would never have taught her that. Only love could teach such a thing, and what did my sister know of love? Nothing but what I could teach her now.

"I won't do it," she said. "I'll live as a crone for the rest of my years, if I must. It's not worth the risk to me."

"Your choice," I said. "But then, what is a magic mirror for? Will you keep me around, feed me magic now and then, keep me safe from breakage, simply to enjoy the pleasure of my company?"

There was a real chance she would see that I was no advantage to her. But only if she was a witch first and a woman—a sister—second.

I waited a long, long moment in which I knew I could not go back to what had been between us. I could not be one of her tools of torture again. I would have to make her destroy me if she could not give up this dark, overlong life.

Then suddenly I felt the barriers come down between us. It was like a rush of fresh cool water on a hot summer's day. And like pure, clean water in a stream, I could taste the magic flowing freely between us. I could float in it, down it, with it, through it. Or I could let it come to me, let it drown me.

Yes, yes. This was the way. I opened myself and was filled again and again until I thought I could take no more. But still she gave.

All this time I had been stealing bits of magic here and there in hopes that I would gain enough. I thought I could buy magic with Minitz's money, but I could never have had this much. I could have laughed at myself for my foolishness, my stingy disbelief of love. I did laugh. I could hear the echo, or was that my sister laughing with me? There seemed to be no more question of whether I would give back to her. The transformation had already begun with her voice. It was hers again now, the voice that she had not changed in all those years, though she had changed everything else.

Once I heard that voice, there was a part of me that lost all fear of her and what she would do when I had done what she asked. I could not doubt my sister, if she had not doubted me. It had always been harder for her to trust, because she had always had so much more to lose. But what had I to lose now?

The magic kept coming and I funneled it back to her unstintingly. The quick work I had done before was now refined. Her hands lost their spots, her skin grew youthfully resilient, the wrinkles around her neck were smoothed out, her stomach tightened, her hips ceased their arthritic clicks. Up and down I went, beautifying and more. That was what she had always wanted, in the past. So I gave it to her again. But I did not stop there.

I found her mind, the lines where memories had been cut off, and restored them. I did not pick and choose between good and bad. Just as I had had to bring them all together, she must do the same. And I could not see her memories of me, whether there were times when I had wronged her. But to return it all to her was surely as much a gift of trust and love as she had given me with her magic. She could hate me now, or not. She could destroy me now or not. I did not know what it would be. But to have my sister back, if only for a moment, was all I asked.

"I love you, Amanda," I said. Then I waited to see if those words were the beginning or the end.

Chapter Twenty-Six

"MIRA," SHE SAID. "I remember."

She picked me up, and I felt tears running down my glass. It was strange. Her features were exactly as they had been, down to the tiniest detail. I could see the shock of white hair over her left ear, too dramatic to let go of, she informed me when it grew there naturally sometime after she was queen. The fingernails she would always have long. The quirk of her eyebrows, one higher than the other when she was in deep thought as she was now.

But there was more than I had meant to put in. I had never seen the hint of wrinkles in her brow or the softening of her lush red lips. Where had the rounded shoulders come from? When had her eyes grown so warmly brown? Had she changed herself as I changed her, with magic? Or was it more than magic?

"After all that I did to you, you did not seek revenge?" she asked.

I could not claim that much goodness. "I did not know you were alive to seek revenge against."

"Ah," she nodded. "I left you there. On the wall, waiting for me."

"One hundred years I waited," I said.

"And then you came to find me."

"Hardly." I would be as truthful with her as Ivana and Talia had been with each other. They had shown me the way. There could only be truth between sisters, sharp as it was. "I came to find myself, to make myself human again. I was drawn to your magic, but I did not know it was you, either. Not until you appeared here, connected to Zerba's old book of spells."

"Then—how—why—?" Confusion filled her face.

"Why did I keep my promise?" I asked.

"I thought there was no reason not to give my magic up. I was tired of it, after all these years."

"It is not what it seems," I said. I had learned that too.

"No. Less—and more." She looked in my glass, and I thought that she would change me then too. "Forgive me, Mira," she said.

But footsteps and shouts interrupted her. They came from behind the orchard gate. I turned and saw Ivana and Talia—and the duke, silhouetted against the outline of the castle behind.

"Do not try your magic here!" the duke shouted. He

held a sword in his hand, and his face was bare to the morning sun. He looked as though he had just woken up and thrown on his boots and his cloak. His eyes were wild.

My sister turned to face him, tucking me behind her back. I think she meant to protect me from him, which was amusing. Talia and Ivana had surely come to protect me from her. But who knew what the duke's reasons were?

"You!" he said. "You are the witch who killed my brothers, aren't you? The witch who destroyed my face and nearly destroyed my chance for happiness in this life."

My sister did not deny it.

I thought of all the memories I had given back to her. What if it had happened too quickly? What if I had overwhelmed her with what she had done and who she had been? She had said she was tired of life before. She must be doubly tired now. But I could not bear to let her go so easily.

"Talia, Ivana, please! There is no need for this."

Ivana flanked the duke, her mouth a grim line, her fists ready to fight for me. Talia held the book of spells in her hand like a weapon she knew how to use.

"We saw her take you from the room," said Ivana. "We know you did not go willingly."

"Her magic kept us still, but we came for you, Mira. Whatever she's done to you to make you help her, we promise we'll change you back." No doubt Talia meant this sincerely, but she was as blind to the truth here as she had been to Blenin on first meeting. She needed more information, but it was too long a story to tell.

"Let her speak for herself, Duke Fensky," I pleaded with the one I knew was the most dangerous here. "Give her a chance!"

"A chance for her to steal another soul?" he asked. There was a cold passion in his speech. "Pray for your own soul now, Witch!"

He lunged with his sword, but my sister slipped away from him. Instead of her heart, he struck into the heart of the crimson apple tree. I could hear the groaning death cry of the soul trapped within, a soul who probably could not have been saved with any amount of magic.

My sister stared at it. "Farewell," she murmured, "and peace."

"My favorite tree." The duke seemed frozen at the thought.

My sister looked at me. Then at the duke. She reached out a hand and the duke moved, more quickly than he ever could have without her magic.

He wrenched the sword from the tree and threw it into my sister's heart. "There is what I think of your magic, in any form," he said as he stood over her.

My sister's face went soft, as it had been when we

first met. Softer, because even then she had been teaching herself to be hard.

She slid to the ground, an arm still tightly clasped around me. I felt her magic streaming out of her as I had felt the life stream out of so many dying creatures before. I did not mean to gather it to myself, but somehow it came to me anyway. A last gift from my sister.

I swelled, heard the glass rushing with blood. And then it broke and I felt arms reaching out of the wood. Not one finger at a time as it had happened before, but my whole arm at once, then the other. And fingers, legs, toes.

I gasped. The air came from my own mouth. I could open it, and close it. I could feel my sister's dying body next to mine.

"Mira?" she whispered.

"Amanda," I said. Then I looked down at myself. I was not the girl I had been. I was the woman I would have become, if I had lived out my life at my sister's side—in human form.

A woman who was more than one hundred years old. A woman who was still too tall, still broad shouldered, and still clumsy in her movements. A woman whose over-large hands were dotted with brown spots, whose olive-colored skin was puckered and sagging everywhere. A woman whose hair was pure white, as white as Zerba's when she had died.

I could have tried to harness the magic that flowed past me, to make myself young again. But instead I let it go by me, to return to the lives of those all around here. It was only fair, I thought, considering how much had been taken from them. The duke would not accept a complete renewal, but if the edge of the horror came off of him—was that wrong?

"Mira, I always loved you," said Amanda. The blood flowed from her chest in a great stream down her, dressing her in the most beautiful crimson gown she had ever worn. "But I was afraid of the power it would give you, if you knew it."

"Yes," I said. "The duke is right, you see. Love is more powerful than magic, isn't it?" I held her hand as she nodded, then gasped, and died. I knew I had only a moment more myself, but I turned to Talia and Ivana.

"Magic is born in death," I said. "But love is born in life, and death cannot end it." It was true for me and my sister, and I hoped it would be true for them too.

Mette Ivie Harrison

studied German in college, which is where she got her taste for the grim side of fairy tales. She currently juggles her time swimming, biking, playing the violin, taking care of five children, and searching for her own magic mirror.

Ms. Harrison lives in Utah. For more information about her and her books, visit:

www.metteivieharrison.com.